This copy of

A Night on Thunder Rock
and other adventure stories
by Enid Blyton

belongs to

_____

_____

A Night
on Thunder Rock

and other adventure stories

SPARROW
BOOKS

A Sparrow Book
Published by Arrow Books Limited
17-21 Conway Street, London W1P 6JD

An imprint of the Hutchinson Publishing Group

London Melbourne Sydney Auckland
Johannesburg and agencies throughout the world

Originally published in Enid Blyton's Treasury
© Darrell Waters Ltd 1947
First published by Evans Brothers Ltd 1947

Sparrow edition 1983

Set in A.M. Baskerville by
Photobooks (Bristol) Ltd

Made and printed in Great Britain
by the Anchor Press Ltd
Tiptree, Essex

ISBN 0 09 932390 7

Contents

1. A Night on Thunder Rock

'Daddy, we've got something to ask you,' said Robert. 'We do hope you'll say yes!'

'Well, I'm not promising till I know what it is,' said Daddy, cautiously. 'I've been caught that way before!'

'It's something quite simple,' said Rita.

'Yes, something you'd love to do yourself,' said Fred. 'It's this – can we spend a night on Thunder Rock?'

Thunder Rock was a tiny rocky island not far out from the coast. The three children had a small boat of their own, and were used to rowing about by themselves. They had often rowed to Thunder Rock and had a picnic there.

'So now you want to spend a *night* there,' said their father. 'Well, what does your mother say?'

'She says we must ask *you*,' said Robert. 'Say yes, Daddy. Only just one night. It would be such fun to camp out there all by ourselves.'

'We'd take rugs and things,' said Rita. 'We'd choose a very fine warm night. It would be wonderful to go off to sleep at night with the waves beating on the rocks round us, and the stars blinking above us.'

'And waking up in the morning with the sun, and slipping into the water first thing for a swim,' said Fred. 'Come on, Dad – say yes.'

'Well, what about that old boat of yours?' said his father. 'I heard it was leaking. Is it safe?'

'Pretty safe, because we can always bale out the water,' said Rita. 'We don't mind. Anyway we can all swim. But I don't think the poor old boat will last much longer, Daddy. Are new boats very expensive?'

'Very,' said her father. 'No hope of getting one, so don't make plans. You'll have to make the leaky old tub do for some time – but mind, if it gets too bad we'll have to scrap it. No good running into danger, and you never know.'

'Well – can we go to Thunder Rock for the night?' asked Fred. 'You haven't said yet.'

His father smiled. 'All right – you can go. Take your food with you, and rugs and things. You'll be all right. It *is* fun to camp out on a little island like that. You feel so very much all on your own.'

'Oh, *thanks*, Daddy! We never thought you'd say yes!'

In delight the three children rushed off to their mother to tell her. 'Well, I do hope you'll all be all right,' she said. 'You're old enough to look after yourselves now – Robert is fourteen and very strong. Don't get up to any silly tricks though. And be sure that old tub of yours doesn't leak too much.'

The children said nothing about their boat. She really was leaking very badly, and needed a lot of baling to keep her from sinking lower and lower! But if only she would last till they had had their night on Thunder Rock!

They made all their plans. Rita fetched a pile of old rugs and old coats. Fred asked his mother for a few tins of meat and fruit to take with them, and some ginger beer. Robert went to get the boat ready. They planned to set off that evening, have a picnic supper, a swim in the sun-warmed water, and then a lovely talk lying on the rugs, looking up to the starry sky.

'It will be gorgeous hearing the waves lapping round all the time,' said Robert. 'Fancy being all by ourselves like that, too. Nobody to send us here and there, nobody to ask what we're up to, nobody to say we're making too much noise!'

They said good-bye and set off in the boat. Everything had been piled in. Had they forgotten anything? No, they didn't think so. Robert and Fred pulled at the oars and Rita baled hard. 'Blow this leak! It's getting worse. I honestly don't think the poor old tub will last much longer.'

'Well, Ted, the fisherman, says she's too old to

mend,' said Robert, pulling hard. 'Say when you're tired of baling, Rita, and I'll have a turn and you can row.' Gulls cried loudly all round them. The sea was very calm, and only a slight swell lifted the boat now and again. The sun shone from the western sky, and the water gleamed blue and purple and green. Lovely!

They got to Thunder Rock at last. They pulled the boat into a tiny cove, out of reach of the waves. Rita took out the rugs and old coats and spread them on a sandy place between some high rocks.

'We'll be well sheltered here,' she said. 'And the sand is warm and soft. Won't it be gorgeous sleeping out here? Now what about supper?'

Supper was lovely. Tinned salmon, tinned pineapple, new bread and butter, chocolate and ginger beer. 'Better than any meal on a table!' said Fred. ''Now let's have a look round Thunder Rock and then have a swim when our supper's settled a bit.'

Thunder Rock was an odd little island. It was nothing but rocks and coves. Nothing grew on it at all, except seaweed. The sea-birds came to it, and liked to stand on the highest rocks, gazing out to sea. They fluttered away a little when the children came near to them, but did not fly right off.

'Lovely things!' said Rita, watching a big gull

alight. 'I wouldn't mind being a gull – swimming, flying, paddling, gliding, diving – what a nice life!'

They had their swim and then lay on their rugs in the twilight, warm and glowing. They put on pyjamas, and then Fred yawned. 'Gosh, are you sleepy already?' said Rita. 'I'm not. I want to enjoy every minute of this exciting evening. Don't let's go to sleep yet.'

'Of course we won't,' said Robert, nibbling a bar of chocolate. 'The sun's quite gone now. There's not a single bit of pink cloud left in the sky. But it's still very warm.'

'The waves sound nice, splashing all round Thunder Rock,' said Rita, looking sleepy. They went on talking for a while, and then Fred gave another yawn, a most enormous one this time.

'I really don't believe I can keep awake,' he said. 'I do want to, but my eyes keep closing. I bet we'll sleep well tonight – with nothing whatever to disturb us except the sound of the sea!'

'All right. We'll say good night then,' said Rita. 'I feel sleepy, too. I'm going to fix my eyes on that bright star over there and see how long I can keep awake. It's so lovely out here all alone on Thunder Rock.'

It was not long before they were all asleep. The stars shone in the sky, and the sea splashed quietly on the rocks. There was no other sound to be heard.

But wait a minute – *was* there no other sound? Robert suddenly woke up with a jump. He lay there for a moment, wondering where he was. How strange to see the sky above him instead of the ceiling of his bedroom! Then he remembered – of course – he was on Thunder Rock. Good!

He was just about to go to sleep again when he heard the sound that had awakened him. It was an extra loud splash – and then another and another. Regular splashes.

Robert sat up. It sounded like a boat being rowed along, not far from Thunder Rock!

Then he heard low voices. That made him stiffen to attention even more. A boat near Thunder Rock – and voices in the middle of the night. What did it mean?

Cautiously Robert awoke Fred and whispered in his ear. 'Don't make a row. There's a boat being rowed to Thunder Rock. I can hear it – and voices too.'

The boys sat and listened. But the boat did not come to Thunder Rock after all. It went right round it and the voices died away. The splash of the oars could no longer be heard.

'The boat's on the landward side of the rock now,' whispered Robert. 'Let's go round and see if we can spot it. There's only starlight to see by but we might just make it out.'

They walked cautiously over the rocks, and round to the other side of the little island. They could see a dark mass some way off – that must be the boat! But who was in it – and why come rowing over the sea at this time of night? Where to? And where from?

'It's all very mysterious,' said Robert. 'Now let's think. Where is that boat heading for?'

'It's going towards the rocky cliffs of the mainland,' said Fred. 'I should think towards the part that is always washed by the sea – the part we've never been able to explore properly because you can't get round to it.'

'There might be caves there,' said Robert. 'I wonder where the boat came from, though. It seemed to come from out at sea – and yet it was only rowed.'

'Do you know – I bet that boat came from some motor launch some way out,' said Fred, suddenly. 'They wouldn't dare to bring it right in, if they were doing anything they shouldn't, because the motor would be heard. I bet the boat left the launch right out to sea – and was rowed in quietly, with some kind of goods. Probably they've come from France.'

'Do you mean *smuggled* goods?' said Robert in sudden excitement. 'Gosh – smugglers!'

'Well, you know there are plenty of smugglers today, now that things are expensive and difficult to get,' said Fred. 'We've heard Mother talking about it with Daddy, I bet you anything you like we've just heard a boat-load of smugglers passing, with smuggled goods in the boat – and they're heading for the cliffs, where they've either got a hiding-place or friends to take the goods from them!'

Robert whistled. He gazed towards the dark land, which could be faintly seen as a black blur in the starlit night. 'Yes. You may be right. Smugglers! What are we going to do about it?'

'Let's go and wake Rita,' said Fred. 'We can talk about it then, all together. Gosh, I feel wide awake now, don't you?'

Rita was very excited when she heard the boys' news. 'You might have wakened me before,' she said indignantly. 'Do you suppose the smugglers' boat will come back?'

'Well – yes – I suppose it may,' said Robert. 'I hadn't thought of that. We'd better keep a look-out.'

They all went round to the other side of the little island, and strained their eyes towards the distant cliffs. Then Robert gave an exclamation.

'Look – I'm sure I can see a light – it must be at the bottom of the cliffs, I should think.'

They all stared hard, and soon Rita and Fred could see a faint light, too.

'I bet that's where the smugglers are, with their goods!' said Robert.

They sat and watched and talked for a long time. The light disappeared. Then suddenly Robert's sharp ears heard something and he clutched Rita and Fred, making them jump.

'They're coming back! Sh!'

And then there came the sound of oars again, and a murmur of voices. The boat passed in the darkness, a blur against the water. The children hardly dared to breathe.

They began to whisper when the boat was out of hearing.

'They must have put the goods in a cave! Let's go tomorrow and find out!'

'Sh! Listen! I believe I can hear a motor starting up a good way out. I bet the smugglers are off back to France!'

'I wish daylight would come. I want to go off and hunt for the smuggled goods!'

But day did not come. It was still only the middle of the night and the children fell asleep again and could hardly believe, in the morning, that anything had happened in the night.

'But it must have, because we all know about it!' said Rita. 'So it can't have been a dream. Let's have breakfast and then go and explore those cliffs. We can row quite near to them.'

So after a meal they set off in their leaky old boat. They rowed towards the towering, rocky cliffs, round whose base the sea washed continually. They came nearer and nearer, and then, when they were afraid of going on the rocks, they rowed round the cliffs, examining every foot of them as carefully as they could.

And they found what they were looking for! They came suddenly to a cleft in the cliff, and guided their boat carefully towards it. A wave took them into the curious crack and they found themselves in an enclosed channel, walled in by steep cliffs, with not much more room than the boat needed for itself.

On one side of the channel was a cave, running into the cliff, quite hidden from the sea outside. 'You hold the boat steady by hanging on to this rock, Fred, and I'll have a look into the cave,' said Robert. He leapt from the boat on to a rock and then peered into the cave. He gave a yell.

'Hey! Stacks of things! Boxes and packages of all kinds. This is where those smugglers put their things. I bet someone on the mainland collects them when it's safe to do so – probably by boat.'

He went back to the boat and got in. 'I'd like to undo some of those things,' he said. 'But I suppose I'd better not. It's a matter for the police now.'

'Is it really?' said Rita, looking rather scared. 'Well, come on, then. Let's get back home.'

They shoved the boat down through the cleft of the cliff back to the open sea again. Robert and Fred took the oars. Fred gave a shout of dismay.

'Hey! You'll have to bale like fury, Rita, the boat's awfully full of water. We'll be swimming soon! Get the baler, quick.'

Certainly the boat was leaking worse than ever. Rita began to bale quickly. The boys rowed hard. But the boat was heavy now with water, and it was difficult going. In the end the boys had to stop rowing and help Rita with the baling.

When they had got the boat a good bit lighter, they took the oars again. 'You'll have to buck up,' said Rita, anxiously. 'It'll fill again directly. It must have sprung another leak. I hope we get back before it fills and sinks!'

The boat began to fill quickly again. The boys rowed hard. Just before they got to shore the boat quietly began to sink beneath them!

They had to get out and wade to shore, carrying what they could of their goods. 'That's very bad luck,' said Robert, sadly. 'I liked that old boat. I'm afraid she's done for now. Come on, let's go home and tell Mother what's happened. Then she can ring up the police.'

Mother was amazed at all they had to tell. She was horrified about the boat, and very glad they had got home safely, though they were very wet.

'I can hardly believe this tale of smugglers,' she said. 'But I suppose I'd better ring up the police. I'll do it now, whilst you go and put on dry things.'

It wasn't long before an Inspector of Police was round in his car. He listened with the greatest interest to all that the children told him.

'I expect they've really hit on something,' he told their mother. 'We know smuggling is going on all round the coast. But it's difficult to trace. I'll get a boat and go round to this cave. Perhaps I could take the children's boat and they could direct me to the place.'

'It's sunk,' said Fred, sorrowfully. 'We haven't got a boat! We feel very upset about it. Ted, the fisherman, will lend you his. We'll come too.'

The Inspector found that the goods in the cave were most certainly smuggled. 'Silk stockings! Bottles of brandy! Perfume of all kinds! My word, this is a haul!' he said in delight. 'Well, we'll remove all these goods tonight when nobody is likely to see us, and then we'll set a watch for the smugglers' friends, whoever they are. They are sure to come to fetch the goods soon. And we will also put somebody on Thunder Rock, lying in wait for the smugglers when they come again, as they are sure to do.'

It all sounded very exciting indeed. The

children wanted to go to Thunder Rock with the watchers, but the Inspector said no. 'There may be danger – shooting, for instance,' he said. 'You're better out of things like that. I'll let you know what happens, don't worry!'

He kept his word, and brought them a very exciting story the next week. 'We've got the men who receive the goods,' he began. 'We caught them rowing round to the cave to fetch them. And now we've got the smugglers too! Three of them!'

'Did you catch them in their boat?' asked Rita.

'We followed their boat when it went back to the open sea,' said the Inspector. 'And there, sure enough was a smart little motor launch waiting for them. We got the whole lot – so *that* spot of smuggling is stopped for a little while at any rate.'

'What a good thing we went to spend the night on Thunder Rock!' said Fred. 'Jolly bad luck our boat is gone, though.'

'Oh, I wouldn't worry about that,' said the Inspector, in an airy voice. 'We want to give you a reward for your help – you'll find it in Ted the fisherman's charge if you care to go and look!'

The children tore down to the beach, and found Ted there, grinning. Beside his boat lay another one, newly-painted and smart.

'Good morning to you,' said Ted. 'Come to

have a look at your new boat? Smart, isn't she? My word, you're lucky children, aren't you?'

'We *are*!' said Rita, in delight. 'Bags I row her first! Oh, what a beauty. Come on, boys – haul her down the beach. Off we go!'

And off they went, bobbing lightly up and down on the waves. They rowed to Thunder Rock, pulled the boat up on the sand and lay down in the sun.

'Good old Thunder Rock!' said Fred, banging the sand below him with his open hand. 'If it hadn't been for you we'd never have got that marvellous – wonderful – super – new boat!'

2. The Mystery of Melling Cottage

'Your Uncle Thomas is coming to stay for a day or two,' Mrs Hollins said to John. 'He's an Inspector, you know, in the police force, and a very clever man.'

'Goodness!' said John. 'Will he tell me stories of how he catches burglars and thieves?'

'I daresay he will, if you ask him,' said his mother. 'But you better behave yourself when he comes! He thinks that boys ought to be taught how to behave when they're young – then, he says, they wouldn't get into trouble when they're older, and appear in the courts.'

John grinned at his mother. He wasn't a bad lad, and he knew his mother was proud of him. 'Well, I'll try not to burgle anybody's house or steal anybody's chickens, Mother!' he said, 'at any rate while Uncle Thomas is here!'

Uncle Thomas arrived. He was not in uniform because he was on holiday and John felt rather disappointed. He had hoped to see a very grand-looking policeman in Inspector's uniform. But Uncle Thomas was in a tweed suit and except that he was very big and had a very clever face with a pair of sharp eyes, he looked quite ordinary.

He liked John at once. 'Now there's a smart lad for you,' he said to John's mother, when the boy was out of the room. 'Asks me sensible questions, listens quietly to my answers, and takes it all in. And when I took him out for a walk this morning he noticed quite as much as I did.'

'I'm glad,' said Mrs Hollins. 'He's a good boy too, honest and straight. I'm lucky!'

John heard a lot of his uncle's tales. How this thief was caught, and that one – how a burglar was traced and the stolen goods found – how criminals are dealt with and punished.

'We learn to use our eyes, our ears, yes, and even our noses, in the police force!' said his uncle. 'You would be surprised if you knew how many times a very small thing has led to the capture of rogues.'

John made up his mind to use his ears, eyes, and even his nose too in future, just in *case* he might happen on something interesting. But although he kept a sharp look-out as he went about, he couldn't really seem to find anything suspicious or odd that needed looking into.

'John dear, take this bundle of old clothes along to Mrs Browning, will you,' said his mother, two days later. 'She's a poor old thing and lives all alone in Melling Cottage. You know where that is.'

'Yes, I know,' said John, and put down his book. 'I'll go now.' He took the bundle of clothes and set off to Melling Cottage. He knew where it was, at the end of a little lane.

On the way he met old Mrs Browning herself. She was a little bent woman, with a pale worried face. She had a basket in one hand, and her purse in the other. She was so thin that John felt sure she didn't eat enough.

'Oh, Mrs Browning, good morning,' said John. 'I was just going to your cottage with these clothes from my mother. Will there be anyone there?'

'No, no, there won't,' said Mrs Browning. 'It is empty, and I've locked the door. I'll take the clothes with me now, thank you, young John, and carry them back home when I've done the shopping.'

'Oh no, they're heavy,' said John. 'Haven't you got a shed or anything I can just pop the bundle into, till you come back? I could run along to your cottage, put the clothes in the shed, and you'd find them there when you got back.'

Mrs Browning hesitated. 'Well, yes, there is an old shed,' she said. 'It's halfway down the garden. You could slip down there, open the door and put in the bundle, John. Thank you very much.'

John said good-bye and went off with the bundle. He came to the deserted lane where Melling Cottage stood. He went down it and saw the little cottage, a tiny wreath of smoke coming from its chimney.

He pushed open the rickety gate and went along the side of the house into the garden. Yes, there was the shed, halfway down. He went to it, opened the wooden door and looked inside. It seemed to be full of rubbish, a broken chair or two, a few pots, a spade, and some firewood. John put the bundle of old clothes down on a broken chair and then made his way up the garden again, towards the cottage.

Growing beside the wall was a very tall foxglove. A bumble-bee crawled into one, and John stood still to watch it. And then, as he was standing there, he heard a sudden noise from inside the cottage.

It was the sound of people talking! It started up quite suddenly and made him jump. Who was in the cottage? Mrs Browning had distinctly said that it was empty and locked up. Then who was there?

The voices went on. Then suddenly they stopped and a band began to play, loudly at first, and then softly.

'What an idiot I am!' said John to himself. 'It's not people. It's only the radio.'

He was about to go on, when a sudden thought struck him. Surely the radio had started up quite suddenly – it hadn't been on when he first stopped to look at the bumble-bee in the foxglove. And then the programme had been switched to another one – well, then there must be someone in the house playing about with it!

It was very puzzling. John wondered what to do. He decided to go and knock at the door and see if anyone came. So he went round to the little front door and knocked hard. He waited, but nobody came. There was not a sound from the cottage except the radio, which was still playing music.

John left the cottage, still feeling very puzzled. He met little Mrs Browning hurrying home from her shopping. She stopped and spoke to him.

'Did you find the shed all right? Thank you, young John, you're kind.'

'Oh, Mrs Browning, I hope there isn't anyone in your cottage,' said John, anxiously, 'because when I was coming back from the shed, I suddenly heard the radio.'

Mrs Browning looked startled. Then she smiled. 'Oh, I left it on when I went out for my bit of shopping. I'm that careless! No wonder it gave you a start, young John. I'm always doing that.'

'Oh,' said John, thinking that he must have

been mistaken. 'Well, that explains it, then!'

He walked back home. But on the way he remembered that he had distinctly heard two programmes, one after the other, as if the radio had first been on one, and then had been switched to another.

He thought about it. 'Perhaps though, it *was* just one programme,' he said to himself. 'I might have heard the end of one talking bit, and then the beginning of the next which was music. It could easily have been one programme. And anyway, Mrs Browning seemed quite certain she had left it going.'

All the same there was a little nagging doubt going on at the back of his mind. It *did* seem as if the radio had suddenly been put on – else why hadn't he heard it when he first went down the garden? He decided to look at the newspaper, and see what programmes were on at that particular time.

It was about ten past eleven when I was there, thought John, looking at his watch. He looked up the programmes. On one there was a talk, lasting from eleven o'clock to a quarter to twelve. On another there was a musical half-hour of dance-band playing.

'Well, then, I *did* hear a bit of *two* programmes,' said John to himself. 'It's very strange. I wonder if I ought to find out a little more? I wouldn't like Mrs Browning to find a burglar waiting for her in her cottage!'

So that afternoon John went along to Melling Cottage again. The smoke was still coming from the chimney. The radio was silent now. There seemed to be no one about at all.

Feeling a little bit uncomfortable John knocked at the door. He heard a sudden scraping noise from inside, and then silence. Somebody was there, no doubt about it. He knocked again. He heard another little noise, this time from upstairs. Then he heard footsteps coming to the door. He held his breath, wondering who was going to open it.

And, after all, it was little Mrs Browning, looking quite scared! 'Oh, John, it's you!' she said, relieved. 'Not many people come along here, and I couldn't think who it was. You must excuse my being so long in answering, but I was in the middle of my cooking.'

'That's all right,' said John. 'I – er – I just came to see if you'd found the clothes all right in the shed.'

'Oh yes, thank you,' said Mrs Browning. 'Won't you come in?'

'Well, I don't think I will,' said John, feeling rather foolish. 'Good-bye, Mrs Browning.'

He went away, still feeling foolish. All the same, he was feeling puzzled too. Why had he heard a noise downstairs when he had first knocked, and a noise upstairs when he had knocked a second time?

I'm making a fuss about nothing! he thought at last. Absolutely nothing. I'll forget about it.

But that night, in bed, he began to worry about it again. He felt sure something was not quite right at Melling Cottage. Mrs Browning did look very white and worried and frightened. She had gone very thin, too. Was there anything the matter?

All at once John threw off the bedclothes, dressed himself quickly, put on his gym shoes and slipped quietly downstairs and out of the back door. He was soon making his way to Melling Cottage. It was about eleven o'clock, and dark, for there was no moon at all.

Down the little lane went John, and came to Melling Cottage. It stood there, a small dark mass by the side of the lane. There was no light in it at all, and no sound from it.

I'm an idiot, thought John to himself. What did I expect to find? *I* don't know! There isn't a thing to be seen or heard. I expect old Mrs Browning is in bed and fast asleep. Well, I'll just creep quietly round the cottage once and then go back to bed. I'm really being very silly.

He walked quietly along the side of the cottage, and then round to the back. There was still nothing to be seen or heard in the black night. John walked softly over the grass at the back of the cottage.

And then he stopped suddenly. He hadn't seen anything, or heard anything – but what was this he *smelt*?

He stood and sniffed quietly. Somebody quite nearby – sitting at the cottage window perhaps – was smoking a very strong pipe-tobacco. John knew it well, because old Taffy the gardener smoked the same, and John had smelt it time and time again when he had sat with Taffy in the shed during the old man's dinner-hour.

And now he could smell that same tobacco being smoked again! It was quite certain it could not be Mrs Browning. It was some man, sitting there quietly in the dark, smoking by himself.

It was all very strange and puzzling. Did Mrs Browning *know* there was a man in her house? She had said she was all alone, a little bent old woman living by herself. Perhaps she didn't know there was a stranger there?

John sniffed the tobacco smoke once more and then turned to go home very quietly. He let himself in at his back door and wondered what to do. Should he go to Uncle Thomas and wake him and tell him? Or would Uncle think he was silly?

'I'd better wake him,' said John. 'Better to be

thought silly than to leave an old woman in danger. That man might rob her!'

So he woke up his uncle. The Inspector roused himself at once, and sat up, alert and wide-awake. He listened to John's odd little tale.

'You did quite right to come and tell me, John,' he said. 'We'll investigate in the morning. There's something strange going on at Melling Cottage, no doubt about that. Sharp work, John!'

'But oughtn't we to do something tonight?' asked John. 'Suppose that man should rob Mrs Browning or hurt her?'

'I don't think we need worry about that,' said Uncle Thomas. 'Get back to bed. We'll tackle it in the morning.'

The next day Uncle Thomas went along to see the local police and make a few enquiries. Then he called back for John. 'Come along with us,' he said. 'Then you'll see what the mystery was.'

Two policemen were with him. Awed and a little scared John went along to Melling Cottage with them and his uncle. They knocked loudly at the door. Mrs Browning opened it. She gave a scream when she saw the policemen.

'Oh! What do you want?'

'Madam, I'm sorry – but we have reason to believe that you are hiding your son, who is wanted for questioning in connection with two armed robberies,' said one of the policemen, 'I have a search warrant here. I must search your house.'

They went in. John stayed outside with his uncle, looking scared. Presently the two policemen came out again – and this time they had a great lout with them, sullen and brutal-looking. Behind came Mrs Browning weeping bitterly.

'He had got a hiding-place under the boards of the bedroom floor, sir,' said one of the policemen to Uncle Thomas. 'He's frightened his poor old mother terribly – made her hide him – and as far as I can make out she's been giving him all her food and half-starving herself.'

'I told him to give himself up,' wept Mrs Browning. 'But he's never done as I told him, never. I was too scared to say anything. I knew he'd be found sooner or later.'

'Oh, shut up, Ma,' said the sullen youth. He was led off between the two policemen. The Inspector stayed to comfort the poor old woman a little, and John looked at her miserably. How awful to have a son like that!

Mrs Browning saw him. She patted his arm. 'You be a good son to your mother,' she said. 'Don't you turn out like my boy. He's been cruel and unkind to me ever since he was so high. I spoilt him, and this is my reward! Oh, Inspector, sir, I didn't mean to do wrong, hiding him like that but I was right down scared of him and what he might do to me.'

'Now, now, don't you worry any more,' said the Inspector. 'You did what you could. You get somebody to come and stay with you for a few days, and we'll sort it all out when you feel better.'

He and John walked home. Uncle Thomas was pleased with his nephew. 'How old are you, John – just gone twelve? Well, I'm proud of you. Good smart work, that. The police have been looking for that young man for some time and have even searched the cottage once before. But he must have heard they were coming and hid in the woods till the coast was clear again.'

'Uncle, I did what you said,' said John. 'I tried to use my eyes, ears *and* nose!'

'You did very well, Detective John!' said Uncle Thomas. 'I shall expect to hear of more cases you have solved in the future!'

3. Smugglers' Cave

Ronnie, Susie and George were all feeling very sad. Not so much because they were going back to their boarding schools in a few days, but because when they next broke up for the holidays, their lovely home, Grey Towers, would belong to someone else!

'*Why* can't we keep it for ourselves?' asked Susie. 'Mother, it's been our home, and Daddy's home, and Grandpa's home, and even Great-Grandpa's home! Why have we got to leave? It ought to be our home too!'

'Well, dear, we're poor now,' said her mother. 'We can't afford to keep up a big place like this, even though it has belonged to us for three hundred years! Our family used to be rich, you know, in your great-great-grandfather's time. But then he offended a friend of the king of that day and he was stripped of all his money and the famous family jewels.'

'*All* of them?' said Ronnie, who had heard this story before. 'I thought, Mother, that Great-Great-Grandpa hid some of his treasure.'

'So the tale goes,' said Mother. 'But I'm afraid I don't believe that now, Ronnie. It would have been found long ago if it had been hidden. Anyway dozens of our family have looked for it and haven't found it.'

'I've looked for it too,' said George, the eldest. 'I've looked everywhere. I thought there might be a secret panel or something somewhere Mother – that led to a hidden cupboard – but I never found anything!'

'And all because long ago one of our family offended somebody, *we've* got to leave the home we love, and go and live somewhere we'll hate!' said Ronnie.

'I do so love Grey Towers,' said Susie. 'Mother, I can't bear to think I'll never come home to it again. I shall go and say good-bye to every single bit of it before I go back to school.'

'Yes, we'd better do that,' said Ronnie. 'We'll go into every room and every corner, so that we'll remember it always. Let's start now. Let's go up to the towers, and look out of the windows, so that we can see all the country round that we know so well.'

'Yes. And we'll even go down to the cellars, and say good-bye to those,' said George. 'Not that I've ever been very fond of them, but I'm not going to miss anything!'

'Well, we'll take Jumpy with us then,' said Susie. 'There might be rats there and I don't like them. Jumpy can chase them for us. He's a good dog for rats.'

They began to say good-bye for the last time to all the places they loved so well – the rounded tower rooms at each end of the house – their own bedrooms, tucked into the roof – their big playroom with its magnificent view of the nearby sea – the long dark landing where they had often hidden to pounce at one another.

'We mustn't leave out anything,' said Susie, dolefully. 'We'll do the cellars last. Where's Jumpy?'

'Jumpy!' called George, when at last they were ready to go down into the dark cellars. 'Jumpy! Come along! We want you to come down and chase RATS! RATS, boy, RATS!'

'And that's about all we *shall* find down in those old cellars,' said Susie, with a shiver. And down the stone steps they went, with Jumpy leaping beside them.

The cellars were deep down under the house. They were dark, and smelt damp and musty. There was no electric light there, so the children had torches. Jumpy didn't mind the dark at all. He rushed here and there, sniffing in every corner for rats.

Old barrels lined the walls. Empty bottles, thick with dust and cobwebs, stood on dark shelves. Wooden crates stood about. It was not a very pleasant place.

There were three or four cellars of different sizes. Nothing of any value was kept there now, because Mother said it was too damp to store things. So it wasn't really a very interesting place after all.

'I don't feel I mind saying good-bye to the cellars, really,' said Susie, flashing her torch round. 'I never liked them much. Ugh, is that a frog!'

'No – a rat! Hey, Jumpy, here's a RAT for you. Rat, quick!' yelled George. Jumpy raced up at once, his tail quivering in delight. The rat shot into the next cellar and Jumpy tore after him. The children followed, flashing their torches.

The rat ran round the cellar looking for a way of escape, but there was none there. It went into the last cellar of all, a place so hung with cobwebs that Susie stopped in dismay, feeling the webby fingers across her face.

'It's spooky in here!' she said. 'I won't go in!'

Jumpy chased the rat to a corner, where a big barrel stood. Then he scraped and whined loudly, trying to get beneath the barrel.

'The rat's found a way out somehow,' said Ronnie, in disgust. 'I wonder if it could have gone under this barrel. Help me to overturn it,

George. That's right – over she goes! There,
Jumpy, is the rat under it?'

No, it wasn't. But there was a dark hole there
and Jumpy suddenly fell down it unexpectedly,
disappearing with a loud yelp!

'Gracious! What's happened to Jumpy?' said
Susie, in alarm. The boys shone their torches on
the floor under the barrel they had overturned.

'There's a round hole there! Where *does* it lead
to?' said George. 'Look, it's had a wooden lid or
something over it at one time – but it's rotted
away. What a funny thing! Jumpy! Are you all
right?'

A doleful wail came up. Jumpy was plainly not
at all happy. He was frightened out of his life!
The boys shone their torches down the hole. Far
down they could see two green eyes gleaming up
at them. It was poor Jumpy, looking up in
despair.

'We'll get a rope and go down and get Jumpy
up,' said George. 'What a funny pit! What can it
be for? We'll go down and see, shall we? Maybe it
was just a hiding-place for a smuggler!'

'Yes, that's it,' said Ronnie. 'We know that
smuggling was carried on here ages ago. Fancy
us never finding this old hole before. Come on –
let's get a rope and rescue poor old Jumpy. What
a row he's making!'

Soon the three children had found a rope and

were back in the dark cellars. Jumpy was still howling mournfully, and the echoes of his doleful voice filled the cellars and made Susie shiver.

'I don't like it,' she said. 'Let's rescue Jumpy quickly and get back into the daylight again!'

'I'd better go down on the rope and tie Jumpy to it, and you must haul him up somehow,' said George. 'Then I'll come up on the rope myself. It's not very far down – only about two metres I should think.'

He let the rope down, after first tying it firmly to an iron hook in the wall. Then down he went, hand over hand to poor Jumpy. The dog was thrilled to see him and barked joyfully.

George stood at the bottom of the hole, and felt for Jumpy's collar. He meant to tie the rope round him in such a way that the others could haul him up without hurting him.

He switched on his torch – and then he gave a loud cry that made the others jump. 'Hey! It isn't just a hole! There's an opening here – it must lead into a passage! Gracious, how exciting!'

Ronnie and Susie almost fell down the hole in their excitement. What! An opening out of the hole! Where *could* it lead to?

'I'm coming down too!' shouted Ronnie and down he went, almost on top of George. Jumpy, happy now that the children were with him, had

pranced out through the opening at the bottom.
George shouted up to Susie.

'Wait a bit before you come down. Let me and
Ronnie get into the opening, or you'll land on
top of us. I'll shout when we're ready.'

Susie waited till he shouted. Then down she
went on the rope too, hand over hand, as she had
been taught to do at gym.

She saw a small opening at one side of the wall
of the hole. She had to bend down to get through
it. The two boys were there, waiting, their
torches switched on.

'It's a passage!' said Ronnie, excitedly. 'See?
There it goes, down and down! Shall we explore
it?'

'Well, of *course*!' said George. 'What do you
think! I'll go first. Let me squeeze by you.
Gracious, isn't it narrow?'

'Now Jumpy's gone again,' said Ronnie. 'He
must be halfway down the passage by now.
JUMPY! Come back, you silly dog, or you'll get
lost.'

A distant bark answered him. Jumpy was
doing a bit of exploring himself! The children
followed, their heads bumping into the rocky
roof of the passage every now and again.

'It's leading towards the sea!' cried Ronnie.
'It'll come out somewhere on the shore, I bet it
will!'

The passage went down and down, sometimes so steep and rocky that the children almost fell. It was all very strange and exciting. Their torches made patches of light in the darkness, and now and again they caught sight of Jumpy's wagging tail some way in front of them.

Ronnie suddenly heard a curious noise. He stopped. 'Listen,' he said, in alarm. 'What's that? Can you hear that queer booming sound? Whatever can it be?'

'I know!' said Susie. 'It's the sea! We're coming near the sea. I wonder what part of the beach we shall come out on. Won't anyone walking on the beach be astonished to see us!'

Suddenly the steep little passage came to an end. In front of them the children saw a huge wooden door, studded with nails, fitting roughly into a rocky archway.

'A door!' said George. 'Fancy finding a door down here! Is it locked?'

It wasn't locked – but it was bolted. Luckily the bolts were on their side of the door! With Jumpy watching impatiently, George and Ronnie tried their best to push back the heavy bolts. They couldn't – but the screws that held the bolts to the door suddenly gave way, for they were set in wood that had rotted and grown weak with the years. They fell out and the door swung open before them.

They flashed their torches beyond it. They saw a cave there, a surprisingly large one, with a high rocky roof and a smooth sandy floor. Directly opposite was a tiny opening, just big enough for a man to creep through, that looked out on the sea just below! It was a most astonishing sight.

Daylight came in through the hole in the cave wall. The children switched off their torches and looked round.

'Old trunks! Brass-bound boxes!' cried Ronnie running to where they stood in untidy heaps here and there. 'Look Susie, look George! Do you suppose they'll be empty?'

'Of course,' said George. He looked round the cave. 'This must have been one of the old smugglers' caves,' he said. 'A jolly well-hidden one too. You can only get into it from the seaward side by that hole there. The smugglers would have to unpack their goods on the moonlit shore, and carry them by hand to that hole, and hand them in to someone ready in this cave.'

'But George – how did these boxes and trunks get here?' asked Susie, looking at them. 'If they didn't come from the shore – they must have come from our house, Grey Towers, years and years ago!'

'Susie's right! They may have belonged to Grey Towers!' shouted Ronnie, and he flung himself down by one of the boxes. 'Quick, let's open them and see what's in them. Oh, quick, quick, quick!'

The children couldn't open the boxes. They must be locked! They were bitterly disappointed. But then, lying half-buried in the sand nearby, George suddenly spied an old bunch of keys!

'We'll try these!' he cried, and was soon busy fitting key after key into one of the trunks. Suddenly one key turned with a grating noise – and George flung open the lid. Packed hurriedly inside, flung in anyhow, were all kinds of jewels! Even now, after all the years of hiding, they gleamed brightly.

'Oh – *look*!' said Susie, in an awed voice, and held up what she felt sure must be an emerald and diamond necklace. 'And look at this – it's like a dog-collar made of rubies. And this – and this!'

'It's the old Grey Towers lost treasure!' said George, and he looked very solemn and yet very excited. 'The treasure our great-great-grandfather must have hidden when he was in disgrace with the king of those days. And somehow nobody can have known where he hid it, and when he was taken away and imprisoned and killed, the treasure stayed here and was never, never found – because nobody ever knew about that little round hole in the cellar under the big barrel!'

After this long speech all the children sat silent, thoughts spinning round in their heads. 'We shan't need to leave our dear old home now! We can stay on at Grey Towers! We can sell all these things and be rich!'

'But will it be treasure-trove? Will the Queen have to have it?' asked Susie, suddenly.

'Of course not. It's our family's riches, even though they've been lost for years!' said George. 'Mother will be pleased.'

'Look what's in *this* box – old gold pieces!' said Ronnie, unlocking another treasure-hoard. 'What a lovely sound they make when I run my hand through them! Let's fill our pockets with this money, and dress ourselves up in all the shining jewels, and go and find Daddy and Mother! We'll make them stare all right!'

This seemed a lovely trick to play, and a fine way to show off their great find. Quickly the children decked themselves out in heavy necklaces, bracelets, brooches, pins, and sparkling belts. They filled their pockets with the money, and took some in their hands to fling down before their parents!

'Let's put that collar of rubies on Jumpy,' cried George, and, giggling with excitement, they did so. Jumpy was astonished by such a heavy collar, but he didn't seem to mind.

Then off they went up the secret passage to the

cellars, shouting and laughing in delight. 'Here comes the old lost treasure! Here comes the old lost treasure!'

And you should have seen their parents' faces when they saw three dirty, dusty, gleaming children arriving with a ruby-collared dog, flinging gold pieces about, and shouting at the tops of their voices.

'We shan't leave Grey Towers after all, we shan't, we shan't!'

And, of course, they didn't!

4. The Wild West Kids

Peter banged on Jill's door early one summer morning. 'Jill! Get up, and let's get the horses. It's a wonderful morning, really sunny.'

Jill sat up with a jump. She looked out of the window. The sun was streaming over the fields out of a sky as blue as forget-me-nots. Hurrah!

'All right, I'm coming,' said Jill and leapt out of bed. 'I'll just throw on my riding breeches and jersey.'

In a few minutes she was down in the stables with Peter. Each of them had a horse of their own, given to them by their grandfather, who was a farmer, and bred cattle, sheep and horses.

'Dear old Bunter,' said Peter, to the lovely chestnut horse that stamped with delight at seeing him so early in the morning. Jill's horse went to her too, nuzzling his great head against her shoulder in the way she loved.

She had called her horse Nuzzler, because of this endearing habit of his. She rubbed her hand up and down his velvety nose. 'Hallo, Nuzzler! Are you pleased to see me so early? What about a gallop?'

Nuzzler whinnied softly, and capered round a

little, his brown eyes gleaming. That was what he loved more than anything – a swift gallop over the grassy hills on a sunny morning.

Then off went both children, first cantering and then letting Bunter and Nuzzler gallop. Peter reined in Bunter a little and then called back to Jill.

'Shall we go to our circus ring this morning? We've got plenty of time. I bet Nuzzler and Bunter would enjoy it.'

'Oh *yes*,' called back Jill. 'I feel as if I could do all sorts of marvellous things on a day like this.'

They galloped to a little round clearing, roughly about the size of a circus ring. Both children had ridden horses since they were five years old and they were as much at home on a horse's back as on their own feet. They had found this little 'circus ring' as they called it, three or four years before, and had practised quite a number of daring tricks there.

Peter stripped off Bunter's saddle. 'I'm going to do bareback riding,' he said. 'Red Indian act! Hooooo, Bunter! Round we go, top speed!'

Bunter knew this trick. Round and round the little green ring he went, just as if he was in a circus. He didn't mind Peter's wild Red Indian yells in the least. He enjoyed them. He even threw back his own head, and gave a loud and exultant neigh, as if he too were whooping like a Red Indian!

Peter stood up on Bunter's back, and stayed there whilst Bunter went round and round. He kept his balance marvellously, and Jill clapped him loudly. Then down he flopped, on to Bunter's back – but rode back to front!

'Jolly good, jolly good!' yelled Jill. 'Now here I come too.'

She galloped into the little green ring and Nuzzler began to go round and round behind Bunter. Jill was as clever as Peter in the way she could stand up on his back. But she could not ride backwards. She always slipped off with a bump when she tried.

As the two children were performing to their heart's content, letting out wild yells at intervals, two boys came up. They also were on horses – and with them was a string of shining, satiny horses, tossing their beautiful heads, and champing their teeth.

Peter and Jill did not see them at first. Then suddenly the two boys cantered into the little green ring on their own horses and joined the private circus! Round and round went the four horses, and Peter and Jill stared in sudden surprise at the newcomers.

'Go on, go on,' yelled one of the boys to Peter, seeing that he was about to rein his horse to a stop.

'Now when I shout – turn your horses the other way and make then canter in the opposite direction.'

He gave a loud shout. 'HUP then!' His own horse and his friend's at once stopped, wheeled their heads round, and tried to go the opposite way. But, of course, Bunter and Nuzzler, not being used to this sudden change, did not turn properly – and all four horses bumped violently into one another. Jill gave a shriek and fell off. Then all four of the children collapsed into laughter.

'Who are you?' asked Peter, looking with admiration at the string of horses standing patiently nearby.

'We're from the circus camp,' said the bigger boy. 'It's arrived this morning, down in Bolter's field over there. We're in charge of the horses. I'm Sam and he's my cousin Dan. Sam and Dan, the world's wonder-riders, real Wild West Kids.'

'Gracious!' said Jill, getting up from the ground. 'Is that what you're called? Are these horses circus horses? Do you ride in the ring?'

'You bet we do,' said Sam. 'We've got proper Red Indian things – and you should hear us yell.'

'Aren't you lucky to belong to a circus?' said Jill, enviously. 'Fancy having all those glorious horses to look after, too. No wonder you ride so well if you perform in the ring.'

'Well, you two kids ride very well too,' said Dan. 'We watched you. Say, your brother's as good as any circus fellow, the way he stands up to ride that horse of his. Has he rubbed any resin into its back so that he doesn't slip? We always do.'

'No. Never heard of it,' said Peter, feeling very pleased at this unexpected praise from a real circus rider. 'We only just mess about, you know.'

'Like to come and see round the circus camp sometime?' asked Sam. 'And can't you come and see us do our act some night? We're hot stuff, Dan and me.'

'We'd *love* to,' said Jill. 'We'd better get back to breakfast now, though. Can we come after that?'

'Right. We'll expect you,' said Sam. 'Come on your horses, of course. They'll enjoy having a gossip with ours.'

Jill and Peter galloped back home, thrilled. 'How wonderful!' said Jill. 'I've always wanted to see round a circus camp. I wonder if they've got elephants this year.'

After breakfast the two galloped off to Bolter's field. It had been quiet and empty the day before but now it was crowded and full of life. Gay caravans stood all about, tents had sprung up, and men were busy putting up the tent in which the circus itself was to perform that night. It was called the big top, and was a most enormous tent.

'*Two* elephants!' said Jill, in delight. 'And look at all those dogs. I've never seen so many tails wagging in my life, not even at a meeting of hounds! What's in that travelling cage, I wonder? Oh, Peter, isn't this fun? I wonder where Sam and Dan are. Let's look for them.'

Sam and Dan were on the look-out for them. They came over to the children and grinned. 'Hallo! So you've come. Leave your horses here with ours, and we'll show you around a bit.'

The circus camp was a thrilling place to wander round. They saw the two enormous elephants, Miss Muffet and Polly Flinders. Polly played a trick on Jill. She suddenly wound her trunk round her waist, lifted her up and set her gently on her head. Jill gave a squeal, half-frightened.

'Hey, Polly! Where are your manners?' called a little man nearby. He walked up, grinning all over his comical freckled face. 'Sorry, Miss, if she scared you. But she only does that to people she really likes. She must have taken a fancy to you!'

He held out his arms and somehow Jill slithered down. She felt proud that Polly had liked her so much, but she thought she would keep away from both elephants, just in *case* they suddenly liked her very much again!

'You must come and see them in the ring some night,' said the little elephant man. 'They're grand. They play cricket with me.'

Someone came swiftly up to them, turning cartwheels in a most graceful and amusing way. Immediately Sam and Dan joined in, and over and over went the three on hands and feet, like living wheels.

'Oh, teach us to do that!' begged Jill, when all three stood upright again, laughing and breathless.

'That's Tickles, the chief clown,' said Dan. He didn't look like a clown at all. He looked like a rather dirty and untidy young man, with a terrific shock of hair, a very snub nose, and the widest grin the children had ever seen. He was dressed in a pullover and old flannel trousers.

'Pleased to meet you,' said Tickles, jumped into the air, turned a double somersault, landed neatly on his feet, and then turned himself upside down and walked about on his hands.

'Full of beans this morning, isn't he?' said Dan. 'He's a scream in the ring. Specially when he tries to ride a horse. We've got one called Toothy, who will try to pick Tickles up whenever he falls off. They bring the house down between them.'

'It does sound exciting,' said Peter. 'I wish I could walk on my hands like Tickles does.'

'Well, we'll teach you if you like,' said Tickles, and walked off with the little company to see an excited crowd of dogs, who were gathering round a small woman.

'That's Madam Lilliput and her performing dogs,' said Dan. 'See that little white one? He's a marvel. They all play football in the ring, and Tippy's goal. You should see him bump the ball away from goal with his nose.'

The dogs looked very lively and well-fed and happy. They jumped up at Madam Lilliput, trying their best to lick her hands. It was plain that every dog adored her.

Taking a big football in her hands, Madam Lilliput wandered off towards the big top. 'She's going to put in some practice in the ring,' said Dan. 'She doesn't like being watched, or I'd take you to see those clever dogs of hers.'

They wandered round the camp, looking at the gay caravans. They peeped inside one or two, marvelling at the amount of stuff that was packed there. All of them looked cosy and comfortable, but one or two were rather dirty and untidy.

'Who lives in that grand motor-caravan?' asked Jill, seeing a big one by itself, painted a lovely blue.

'Oh, that belongs to Jo Martini. He owns the circus,' said Dan. 'He's a fine fellow, but, oh!

what a temper! You'll see him in the ring when you come, with his outsize whip. You'll hear him cracking it, too. It makes a simply terrific noise.'

'Do you remember when we had that bad fellow here – what was his name – Jeremy Hiyo – and. . . .'

'Oh, *yes*,' finished Dan, 'and Jo flew into a temper with him and chased him all round the camp, cracking his great whip so cleverly that the end of it flicked Jeremy each time. Didn't he yell?'

'I've felt the end of that whip myself,' said Sam. 'Makes you yell all right! Look out – there's Jo himself.'

A great big man came out of the blue caravan. He wore spotless white riding breeches and a top-hat. In his hand he carried the biggest whip that Jill and Peter had ever seen. He cracked it, and it went off like a pistol shot. The children jumped. Jo grinned at them.

'Good morning. Visitors, I see. Want to join my circus?'

'Oh! I wish we *could*!' said Jill, fervently. 'But I don't expect we'd be allowed to.'

'I don't expect so either,' said Jo. 'You have to be born to circus life if you're to be any good, you know. Trained to it from a day old. See this whip? You wouldn't believe how often I've used it on these two bad lads here.'

Sam and Dan laughed. Mr Martini cracked his whip again and strode off. 'Isn't he grand?' said Jill. 'I feel half scared of him, but I like him all the same.'

'That's what all the circus folk feel about Jo Martini,' said Sam. 'He's a proper ring-master, he is – strict and stern, not afraid of using his fists and his whip, too, if anyone needs them – but kind as your own mother at home.'

Peter and Jill spent the whole morning in the camp, seeing every animal and person there. The circus folk were friendly and kindly, and the animals all seemed to be treated as if they were humans. There was a big bear there that belonged to one of the clowns, and he was so tame that he was allowed to wander about loose. There were monkeys, too, that leapt and chattered on the roofs of the caravans, pointing at Jill and Peter with little hairy fingers.

'They're surprised to see you,' explained Dan. 'They love anything strange or new. Look out for Scamp – the one over there wearing a little red hat. He's a real ball of mischief. He ran off with Jo's whip one day, and stuck it in the chimney of Tickles' caravan.'

'Look – there's Madam Lilliput coming out of the big tent with her dogs,' said Peter. 'Has she finished practising? Can we go and see the ring?'

'Yes. And it's time we took the horses in and

gave them a bit of practice there, too,' said Sam. 'We've got a new horse, Ladybird. She's not quite sure how to waltz yet.'

Jill and Peter helped the boys to take the horses into the great ring. Sawdust was scattered in the centre. The ring was enclosed by curved pieces of wood covered with red plush. Each piece fitted against the next, and made a great red circle.

It was fun seeing the horses canter round in rhythm, nose to tail. At a shout each turned round slowly and carefully and then went the other way. Then they had to waltz. Sam started a great hurdy-gurdy going, and when the music poured out, every horse pricked up its ears.

'They love music,' said Sam. 'Now watch them waltz to it!'

Most of the horses managed to dance gracefully round and round, turning themselves neatly at the right moment. Jill and Peter watched in amazement. If only Bunter and Nuzzler could do that!

'See the new horse Ladybird – she's trying her best to do what the others do,' said Sam. 'She's going to be a clever little thing.'

'They're all beautiful,' said Jill. 'Absolutely beautiful. Do they wear feathery plumes at night?'

'Yes. They're as grand as can be,' said Sam.

'And don't they love being dressed up too! Bad as the monkeys. They just love it.'

'Now you can see our Wild West act!' said Sam. The string of horses trotted docilely out of the ring. Then in galloped Sam and Dan, whooping and yelling for all they were worth. The things they did! Jill and Peter watched in amazement.

They stood up, they sat down, they slithered right under their horses and up the other side, they stopped at top speed and reared up alarmingly, they even leapt to one another's horses and changed places.

Jill and Peter got tremendously excited and yelled loudly. Then suddenly two brown noses appeared at the tent opening, and Bunter and Nuzzler, attracted by the yells of Jill and Peter, looked in.

'Bunter! Come on! We'll join in!' yelled Peter, and Bunter trotted over to him. Nuzzler came too. In a trice both children were on their horses and in the ring as well. What a commotion there was! The four horses enjoyed it as much as the children, and soon Peter began to do things as daring as those the two boys did. When he jumped from his own horse to Sam's, Dan gave a yell.

'Look at that! Bravo, bravo!'

At last, tired out, and trembling with excitement, all four of them slowed down, and trotted their horses out into the sunshine. Sam and Dan looked admiringly at Jill and Peter.

'You'd be as good as we are, if you did a bit of practising.'

'Do you think so?' asked Peter, eagerly. 'Could we come along and practise with you sometimes? We've got holidays now. Bunter and Nuzzler would love it.'

'Yes, you come,' said Sam. 'Then if you're ever out of a job you could always ask Jo for one in his circus!'

Jill and Peter cantered off, their eyes shining. 'What a morning!' said Peter. 'We've always enjoyed messing about in our own little ring – but to practise in a *real* circus ring – it's marvellous!'

'It's great,' said Jill. 'I do hope Mother won't say no.'

Mother asked a lot of questions, but she didn't say no. 'You'll get tired of it after a day or two,' she said. 'But I've no doubt it will do you good to see how hard the circus folk have to work. *You* just train your horses for fun and pleasure – to the circus folk it is a way of earning a very hard living.'

So, morning after morning Jill and Peter rode down to Bolter's field, where the camp lay set in its circle of gay caravans. They practised hard with Sam and Dan. Nuzzler and Bunter seemed to love it. Nuzzler even managed to learn to waltz quite well, but Bunter couldn't seem to. He *would* turn round the wrong way, and upset all the others.

Sam and Dan taught the children how to turn cartwheels and somersaults. Once they lent them old Red Indian suits, with shaggy trousers, embroidered tunics, and great feathered head-dresses. Jill had never felt so grand in all her life.

'Let's make up a new Red Indian game,' said Sam, suddenly. 'You can be a squaw, Jill, belonging to Peter. We'll be enemies and capture you. We'll tie you up to a tree, and then shoot at you with arrows – then up can come Peter. We'll snatch you up, put you on our horse, and ride off. Then Peter can come thundering behind and rescue you.'

Feeling a bit doubtful about all this, Jill consented. It was certainly exciting, if a bit uncomfortable. She made a very realistic prisoner, yelling and screaming for help so loudly that Tickles the clown looked into the ring to see if she really meant it. He stayed to watch, applauding loudly.

When Peter thundered up on Bunter, and rescued Jill from Sam's horse, everyone was too excited for anything. 'If only we could do that in the ring at night!' said Sam, wiping his hot face. 'Wouldn't everyone love it!'

'Oh dear – I was half afraid I was going to fall off your horse, Sam, before Peter rescued me,' said Jill, sitting down on the red plush ring. 'Goodness, I'm hot. Oh, Nuzzler darling, don't breathe so heavily down my neck. Look, Sam, he's worried about me. He thinks it was all real, not acting!'

So he did. He hadn't been in the game, and he couldn't bear to hear Jill yelling for help. Now he was nuzzling her lovingly, trying to find out if she was all right.

'Horses are the nicest things in the world,' said Jill, stroking Nuzzler's long nose.

'Madam Lilliput wouldn't agree,' said Dan. 'She thinks there's nothing to beat dogs.'

'And the elephant man adores Miss Muffet and Polly Flinders,' said Sam. 'He's always saying that elephants are the cleverest animals in the world.'

'And I suppose Miss Clarissa thinks her monkeys are the best,' grinned Peter. 'Well, give me horses and anyone else can have the rest as far as I'm concerned.'

Both children had been to see the circus show two or three times. How different the circus folk looked when they were all dressed up for the ring! They were grand and gay and beautiful. Madam Lilliput, in her short, sparkling skirt, and her plume of ostrich feathers looked like a beautiful doll, though she was the plainest little woman imaginable in real life. Tickles, the clown, and his friends, Spick, Span and Soapy, the other clowns, looked lively and amusing in their circus clothes – quite different from the rather dirty, untidy youths they were in daily life.

As for Mr Martini, he was really magnificent. He was dressed in gleaming white from top to toe, and even his top-hat was white. His boots were white and so were his riding-breeches. His whip had a vivid scarlet bow, and how he cracked it! He looked wonderful as he stood in the middle of the brilliant ring, with his performers around him.

'You know, Sam, I'd give anything to go into the ring just once,' said Peter, longingly. 'Just to *feel* what it's like – to be one of you, and one with all the animals. There can't be anything like it in the world.'

'There isn't,' said Sam. 'It's the finest feeling there is. In the ring we're all one big family together, doing our best. We may quarrel outside in the camp, but in the ring we're the circus, we're pulling together, we're making a grand show, and aren't we proud of it!'

'I shall be awfully sorry when you go,' said Jill, with a sigh. 'You're all such fun. And those lovely, lovely horses. I know every single one of them now, and I don't know which I like best.

Ladybird, perhaps, because she is so sweet and tries so very, very hard to do as well as the others do.'

'We're giving our last show on Saturday night,' said Sam. 'Then we go on to our next camp. It'll be a grand show, so be sure you come. Jo says he'll give you two of the best seats that Saturday.'

'Of course we'll be there,' said Peter. 'Mother and Daddy are coming too, but they won't want to be in the front. Mother doesn't like to be too near. Lots of children from our school are coming too, so be sure to do your best.'

'You bet!' grinned Sam. 'We'll yell to you when we gallop by in our Wild West act.'

'We've told everybody about you,' said Jill. 'Simply everybody. They'll all be looking out for you and they'll clap you like anything.'

'They'll think you're fantastic,' said Peter. 'I wish they could see *us* performing too – we're almost as good as you are now!'

Saturday morning came. Peter and Jill rode down to the camp, feeling rather sad. It wouldn't be there the next day. It would be on the road, rolling away to another field. How they would miss Sam and Dan and the horses!

'Good thing that school begins again next week,' said Peter. 'I should feel lost without anything to do. What fun we've had!'

When they got to the camp they noticed something odd. There did not seem to be anyone about. Where could they be?

'What's happened to everyone?' said Jill, in wonder. 'Oh look – there's somebody coming out of the big top.'

It was Madam Lilliput coming out of the great circus tent, hurrying as fast as she could. When she saw the two children, she ran towards them, her face screwed up as if she was crying. When she came nearer, the children saw to their horror that tears were running down her cheeks.

'What's the matter? Oh, what's happened?' cried Jill, scared.

'It's Sam,' said Madam Lilliput. 'He climbed up to the top of the tent to put the lamp straight there – and he fell. Oh, poor, poor Sam! What shall we do? We want a doctor, quickly.'

Jill's heart went cold. Sam! Gay, lively, kindly Sam. Tears came into her eyes.

Peter sat still on his horse. Sam had fallen from the top of the tent down to the ring below. He must be very badly hurt indeed.

'Listen,' he said. 'Our father is a doctor. I'll ride back home and get him to come at once. He'll be here in no time. Don't move Sam till he comes.'

The boy flew off like the wind on Bunter. Jill heard the thud of the hoofs as he went, but she did not go with him. She wanted to see poor Sam.

She slipped off her horse and walked on trembling legs to the big circus tent with Madam Lilliput. Everyone was inside, even the dogs and the monkeys. In the centre of the ring lay poor Sam. His eyes were shut and he was as white as paper. Mr Martini was kneeling over him, almost as white as Sam himself. Tickles, the clown, was trying to keep everyone back.

'Don't crowd round,' he said, in a shaky voice, not a bit like his own. 'Give the poor lad a bit of air, can't you?'

Madam Lilliput went up to Mr Martini. 'Jo! There's a doctor coming. Best not move the lad at all. Give him something to drink – a drop of brandy. Peter's gone for his father, who's a doctor.'

The circus folk looked immensely relieved. To them a doctor was a kind of magician who could cure anything. They had been as frightened as children when they heard of Sam's fall, but now they cheered up and murmured the magic words to one another. 'Doctor's coming! Now our Sam will be all right.'

Jill wasn't so sure. She had heard her father talk many times of illnesses and accidents, and she was afraid that Sam might be seriously damaged, perhaps for life.

'Poor, poor Sam! Suppose he can never ride

again! And poor Dan too! He's so fond of Sam, and they do such wonderful things together. And there's tonight too – the last night of all, when they'd planned to put on such a fine show. What a terrible bit of bad luck!'

Peter had found his father about to set out on his rounds in his car. He turned his car round at once, and set off in the direction of the circus. He knew all about Sam and Dan from his children. He was at the camp in four minutes, and drove his car into the field through the gate, bumping over the ruts.

Then he was in the big tent, making his way through the anxious folk. 'Turn them all out,' he said to Jo. 'Every one of them.' And out they went. Jill and Dan were allowed to stay, with Jo – and in a little while Madam Lilliput stole back to see if she could help.

Sam opened his eyes and groaned. Peter's father examined the boy quickly and carefully. Then he stood up.

'He'll be all right, thank goodness. He's not damaged himself too much. He'll have to go to hospital, and have treatment for some time – and he'll be very sore and bruised for a few days. There'll be no riding for him for a month or two, though.'

Tears ran down Dan's face – a curious mixture of tears, really. He was crying for joy because

Sam wasn't seriously damaged – and for grief because now he wouldn't be able to ride with Sam for a long time. Jill sniffed too. She knelt down by Sam and stroked his hand.

'You're not too badly hurt, Sam,' she said. 'You'll be all right. Poor old Sam!'

Sam tried to say something and couldn't. He looked very worried indeed. He tried again.

'What is it, old son?' asked the doctor, gently. 'Don't worry about anything. You won't do yourself any good if you do. Things will be all right.'

'It's tonight,' said Sam, with an effort. 'See? It's the big show tonight. What about – the Wild West Kids?'

'That's all right,' said Jo. 'We'll do without them.'

'No,' said Sam. 'No. There's Dan. Don't leave him out. Jill, you and Peter – can't you do it with Dan?'

'Now don't worry yourself like this,' said the doctor, anxiously. But Jill pulled at his arm.

'Daddy! Why *shouldn't* Peter and I help Dan tonight in the ring? We know everything! We've practised it time and time again. Even Sam says we're as good as he and Dan are!'

Peter was now back, and he joined in eagerly. 'Yes, Dad – we can do the Wild West act. We've got a very good one, with Jill as a squaw.

You've seen it too, haven't you, Mr Martini?'

Jo nodded. He had come into the ring once whilst the four of them were doing it, and had been amused and astonished. He looked at Peter's father.

'They're good,' he said. 'And if it would set Sam's mind at rest – and if *you* wouldn't mind, sir, why I'd be pleased to give your kids a chance in the ring. They'd love it – it would be a reward to them for all the practising they've done with Sam and Dan here. But it's for you to say, sir.'

The doctor looked down at Sam. The boy's eyes were shining and colour had come back to his face. He caught hold of the doctor's hand feebly. 'Give them a chance, sir,' he begged. 'Let the show go on just the same without me, but with Dan and Peter and Jill. I'll feel happy then.'

'All right,' said the doctor, and Peter and Jill looked at one another with shining eyes. Poor Sam – it was because of him they had their chance, and they were immensely sorry for him – but they could not help feeling excited and happy to think of the coming night.

'We'll do our best, Sam,' said Jill, and the boy nodded, looking happy.

'Help me to lift him gently to my car,' said the doctor to Jo. 'I'll take him to hospital myself. You can come with us, Dan. Not you, Jill and Peter.

That would be too big a crowd for Sam. I'll look after the boy, Martini, till he's right, and keep you posted about him.'

'Thanks, sir,' said Jo, gratefully. 'He's got no father or mother. There's only me and I'm his guardian. He's a good lad. Aren't you, Sam?'

Sam tried to put on a grin. He was in pain and it was difficult, but he managed a faint one. Then he was carried gently to the car, and laid comfortably on the back seat.

That evening the three, Dan, Jill and Peter, were in a state of the greatest excitement. Dan, wild and lively after the shock and grief of the morning, shouted and laughed. Peter and Jill dressed themselves in their Red Indian clothes, and Jill found that her hands were shaking with excitement. She could hardly do up her tunic.

All the circus folk came to wish them luck. 'It's grand of you to step in like this, so that Dan can carry on,' said Tickles. 'Our last show in a place is always the best. You'll be fine!'

'I hope so,' said Peter, feeling suddenly nervous. 'You know, Tickles, all our school friends will be there. Can't think what they'll say! And Mother and Daddy are coming too. I hope we don't do anything silly.'

'You'll be all right,' said Tickles. 'We shall all be fine tonight. We're all feeling glad that Sam isn't hurt too badly. He'll be back again before the winter, as good as ever, your father says. Say, he's a grand fellow, your father, isn't he? If I wasn't a clown, I'd be a doctor. Next best thing to making people laugh would be to make them well when they're ill. I wouldn't mind being a doctor at all!'

Peter smiled. Funny old Tickles. Then he began to worry about his part in the show again. Would he really be able to do it all right? Would Bunter be nervous?

Neither Bunter nor Nuzzler were nervous. They were excited and happy. Somehow they sensed that for once they were one with all the other horses. They were THE CIRCUS. Bunter whinnied a little, and Nuzzler nuzzled against him.

The grand parade began to the lively strains of the band. Into the ring went every performer, both human and animal, parading round in their finery, lifting their hands to greet the clapping audience. And into the ring went Jill and Peter too on Bunter and Nuzzler, following Dan. The children were all dressed in their Red Indian things, ready for their act later on. Their hearts were beating fast. They waved their hands too, and tried to see the faces of their parents in the vast audience.

'Hey, there's the Wild West Kids!' shouted a

shrill voice. Peter knew that voice. It belonged to Tubby, a boy in his form. 'Hey, look! There's three of them, not two, tonight.'

Peter waved his hand to Tubby. Tubby did not recognize him in his Red Indian clothes, but he was thrilled that one of the Wild West Kids had actually waved to him.

'See that?' he said proudly to his companions. 'He waved to me. Gosh, wouldn't I like to be in his shoes tonight!'

The grand parade was over. The show began. In came the beautiful horses to canter round and round, and to waltz and do their tricks. How they enjoyed every moment! Everybody clapped wildly at the sight of the sleek shining creatures, and Mr Martini cracked his whip, and looked at them proudly. This was his great moment. He was the grand man of the circus, the ringmaster, and these beautiful horses were his. He wouldn't have changed places for anyone on earth at that moment.

'Good old Jo!' whispered the watching circus folk to one another.

'Crack!' went his whip, and the horses changed round and went in the opposite direction, whilst the band kept time to their cantering.

One after another the turns came on. Tickles and the clowns sent the audience into fits of laughter. They had never been so funny before. When Tickles tried to ride a horse and fell off bump every time, Tubby and the others from Peter's school cried with laughter. It made Jill and Peter laugh to see them.

The elephants played cricket with their trainer, and the dogs played football with Madam Lilliput. Their eager barking filled the ring, and when the little goalkeeper dog saved goal after goal the audience went quite mad with admiration!

'What a fine show!' said Tubby to the others. 'What's next? Oh, the Wild West Kids. Good!'

And into the ring rode Dan, Jill, and Peter! As soon as the time came for them to appear, all their nervousness went. Instead they were filled with a wild excitement, and they galloped in, whooping and yelling for all the world as if they really were the reddest of Red Indians!

The children in the audience clapped and stamped vigorously. This was what they liked. They shouted and yelled as much as the Red Indians did, when they saw the tricks they performed.

Round the ring they went at top speed. Then up on the horses' backs they all stood. Then down they sat, facing their horses' tails. Yes, even Jill could manage that now without sliding off.

Then up they stood again, and Peter and Dan changed horses by jumping from one to the other.

'Good gracious!' said Peter's mother to his father.

'I didn't know they could do *this* kind of thing! Is it safe? Oh my goodness, there they go again. Well, I *never* thought Peter and Jill would go careering round a circus ring, performing like that!'

Then the three did their Red Indian act, where Jill was the squaw. Dan rode off with her and then tied her up to a post. He shot arrows at her, missing her cleverly, and she screamed so realistically that her mother almost went into the ring to rescue her herself!

Then up thundered Peter, whooping for all he was worth. How the audience cheered him! Dan snatched at Jill, got her on his horse, and galloped off with her round the ring. After him went Peter, whirling a lasso, which was another trick he had learnt. He neatly lassoed Dan and drew him to a standstill.

Then he snatched Jill off Dan's horse, put her on his, and rode off with her at top speed, whilst Tubby and the rest cheered frantically at the tops of their voices.

Dan rode out of the ring after Peter. But in a trice they were back again with Jill to take their bows. They leapt off their horses, and bowed time and again. Then they all did a series of cartwheels round their horses, leapt to their feet and vaulted on to their horses' backs. Off they went out of the ring to a perfect tornado of applause.

Their parents clapped madly too. They could not believe that Jill and Peter were so good. As for the circus folk they crowded round them and slapped them on the back till they were sore. Mr Martini strode up and held out his great, hairy hand.

'Fine, fine! Bravo! Best act I've seen any kids do for years! If ever you want a job, you two, come along to me and I'll give you one in my circus. See? If your father and mother ever turn you out of house and home, you'll know where to come to!'

'Thanks, sir,' said Peter, glowing, 'but I don't think that's likely to happen somehow. All the same – it's a great feeling to go into the ring and I'll never, never forget it!'

They stayed behind to have supper with the circus folk, and their mother and father came too. After supper the camp was to start on its journey to its next camping place. It was to travel in the quiet of the night. The moon was bright, the roads were empty. In an hour's time the cara-vans would be on their way, and the lorries would follow after, packed with all the circus properties.

'So it's good-bye,' said Mr Martini, at the end of the hilarious meal. He held out his hand. 'Pleased and proud to have met you. Good as any circus kids you are, and that's saying a lot. Good-bye. Look after Sam for me, and send him back as soon as he's fit.'

All the good-byes were said. Jill and Peter could not help feeling a little sad as they shook hands with Tickles, the elephant man, Madam Lilliput and the rest. They patted all the horses, shook paws with the monkeys and with the performing dogs too.

'We'll come back next year,' said Mr Martini, getting into his blue caravan. 'See you then. And maybe you can do a Wild West act again, with Sam and Dan, if your people will let you. Good-bye!'

The line of caravans crawled out of the field-gate and on to the road. The moon shone down on the gay little houses on wheels. Dogs barked and the two elephants, who were walking, trumpeted loudly.

'They're saying good-bye too,' said Jill. 'Oh Peter – do you think Tubby and the rest will believe it was us, when we tell them next week at school?'

'We'll see,' said Peter with a grin. 'Old Sam

will be thrilled when he hears about it, won't he?'

The next week Peter spoke to Tubby and the others at his school. 'Did you see the circus on Saturday? Did you like it?'

'Oh boy! Did we like it! It was super, colossal, fantastic!' said Tubby, beaming. 'Why, weren't you there? Come to think of it, I didn't see you.'

'Yes. We were there,' said Peter, grinning. 'You saw us all right'.

'I didn't,' said Tubby. 'I looked all round for you. You ought to have gone, you really ought.'

'What did you like the best?' asked Peter. And, of course, he got the answer he hoped for.

'The best? Why, the Wild West Kids of course!' cried Tubby, and the others yelled in agreement. 'You ought to have seen them, Peter – they were GREAT. I'd have loved to be them, wouldn't you?'

'Yes, I would,' said Peter, grinning still more widely. 'And what's more, I *was* one of them. What do you think of *that*, Tubby!' And he gave such a wild Red Indian yell that everyone jumped. Then he did six cartwheels round the classroom, and ended up by colliding with the headmaster who was just coming in at the door.

'Now, my boy! Do you imagine that you are a circus performer?' said the head, sarcastically.

And Peter answered at once. 'Well, yes sir – I do!'

5. Number 62

Ever since John had solved the mystery of Melling Cottage he had been on the look out for another. But mysteries didn't seem to come along very often – and some mysteries turned out not to be mysteries after all!

There was the time when he had seen a man and a woman quarrelling in a garden, and suddenly the man flashed out a knife . . . but when John yelled out that he was going for the police, it turned out that the two were only rehearsing their parts in a play.

John had felt very foolish over that. And another time he had reported a mysterious sack on the other side of a hedge, apparently full of stolen goods. But it was only a sack of potatoes left there by the farmer for his brother to fetch as he passed by on his way to market.

I'd better be careful next time, thought John to himself. I won't report anything unless I'm absolutely sure about it.

Now one afternoon he went by himself to Oaktree Wood. There was a big tree there he liked to climb. It was an easy one, and he could get almost to the top. From the top he could see a very long way indeed.

It was like being in a ship, because the wind swayed the tree, big as it was, and the movement was like a boat going over waves. John liked it. If he shut his eyes he felt as if he were right out at sea.

So this afternoon up the tree he went. He was soon at the top, looking out over the countryside, which lay smiling in the summer sunshine.

John had a book with him. He opened it, settled himself comfortably on a branch and began to read. Sometimes he looked out from his high perch, and saw the lorries, buses and cars going along the roads.

He saw a car stop and pull off the road on to the grass verge. A man got out and disappeared. John waited idly for him to come back, but he didn't. Surely he hadn't gone for a picnic all by himself? John went on reading his book, occasionally glancing up to see if the car was still there.

After half an hour the car was still pulled up, empty. John began to wonder about it. Then he suddenly heard the crack of a twig in the wood below, as if someone had trodden on one and broken it.

There's somebody coming through the wood, thought John, and glanced down through the leaves. But the tree was too thick for him to see anything below on the ground.

He heard a match struck. Somebody was lighting a cigarette. Perhaps he was waiting for someone? John heard a slight cough down below. The man was under the tree. Another twig cracked.

Then there came the sound of someone making his way through the bushes, and a low voice said, 'That you, Lou?'

'Yes,' said the man under the tree. 'Number 62, tomorrow.'

'Okay,' said the other voice and its owner made his way back through the bushes again. That was all. Not another word was said. The man under the tree went off, and in about ten minutes' time John saw him come out of the wood and get into the car.

John strained his eyes to see the number of the car. He could make out the first two letters – ST, and the last figure, which was 0, but that was all. He wrote it down in his notebook.

'Car number ST . . . 0,' he wrote. 'Red in colour. Sports saloon. Can't see make.'

John often wrote things of this kind down but as a rule they were all wasted. Still, you never knew. Things might come in useful sometime. He began to think about the strange message the man under the tree had given to the other, who was, apparently, already hidden in the wood.

'Number 62, tomorrow.'

What did it mean? What was number 62? And why tomorrow? John frowned, and puzzled over it. Should he report what he had seen and heard? No, better not. It might be nothing again.

'Perhaps number 62 is a house somewhere they mean to burgle,' thought John, suddenly. 'Number 62. Where is there a number 62? It must be a fairly long street if there are over sixty houses in it. I'll go and do a little exploring.'

Before he slid cautiously down the tree, he listened to see if anyone might be about – the man hiding in the wood for instance. But he could hear nothing, so down he went, as quietly as he could. Once on the ground he sped through the trees as if he were a rabbit with a dog after him!

He went to the village. There must be a number 62 somewhere. What was the longest road? Yes, Summers Avenue must be. He went along it, looking for 62.

'41, 43, 45 – oh, these are the odd numbers. I want the evens.' He crossed the road and came to the evens.

'42, 44, 46 – blow, there are only two more. 48–50. There's no 62.'

He went down another street but there were even fewer houses there. That was no good. Then he went to Limmers Street, which was a terrace of small houses. Ah, there was a 62 – good! John looked hard at it.

Nobody would want to rob a tiny house like that, surely! Two or three children were playing on the doorstep. No, this couldn't be the 62. That was quite certain.

'Well, there's only the High Street left then,' thought John, and went there. However, he felt that 62 could hardly be the one meant by the man, for it was the Police Station! It had no number, of course, but as it stood between shops labelled 60 and 64, it was clear that it must be 62, if it had a number at all!

'I can't understand it,' said John, puzzled. 'There are only two 62s – and one's a tiny little house and the other's the police station. Perhaps the 62 doesn't mean the number of a house at all.'

Should John go to the police now, and tell them what he had heard? No, he still didn't want to, because it just might mean nothing, and he would be laughed at.

He turned to go home. As he went he saw a man running by in white singlet and shorts. Then after a while another came. They were practising running for races. John stared at them idly. Then he stiffened. Each man had a number on, in big black figures! The first man's number was 14. The next man's was 34. Then came a third man, padding along – he was 53.

John looked after the runners. Could the number 62 belong to one of these runners? Was it a *man*, number 62, that that fellow was talking of? If so, *why*?

He went on towards his home, thinking hard. Daddy was at home. Perhaps he would be able to tell him about the runners, and their big race.

Yes, his father knew all about it. He had been a fine runner in his time, and he told John that there was to be a ten mile race the next day, on a certain route, and that so far as he knew almost a hundred competitors were entered for it.

'Then there may be a number 62' asked John.

'Yes, of course. But why do you ask that?' said his father.

'Oh – I was thinking of something,' said John. 'Daddy, is there a list of the competitors up anywhere? I'd like to have a look and see if I know any of them.'

'Yes. If you go along to the Athletic Club Room, you are sure to see a list there,' said his father. 'I didn't know you were so interested in running!'

John smiled and went off. He found the

Athletic Club Room and peeped in. The secretary was there. 'What do you want, youngster?' he asked.

'Could I just look at the list of runners?' said John. 'For the big race tomorrow?'

'Yes, it's over there,' said the secretary, and pointed with his pen. 'They start at Beamers End, each running two minutes after the last. And they end at Longfields Club Room.'

'Er – do they run past Oaktree Wood?' asked John. The secretary nodded. John began to look down the list of names. He came to number 62.

'62. Laurie Baxter.' Who was Laurie Baxter? He looked at the address. '16 Renfrew St.' That was a street in the next town, near the big factory.

'Laurie Baxter, 16 Renfrew St.' Now why in the world should anyone want to bother about Laurie Baxter running in a Marathon Race?

'Who will win, do you think?' asked John. 'Laurie Baxter?'

'Good gracious, no,' said the secretary. 'He'll be about halfway. He's not much good.'

'Oh well – thank you very much,' said John and went out. Now, was he right or wasn't he, in thinking that Laurie Baxter was the number 62 that the man in the wood was telling the other fellow about, for some reason or another? And was he right in thinking that the fellow in hiding was going to lie in wait for Laurie Baxter? If only he knew!

He couldn't possibly go to the police and say 'I think that Laurie Baxter, in tomorrow's race, will probably disappear halfway through, and not turn up at the end because somebody in Oaktree is lying in wait for him!' It sounded too silly for words – and it might not be true. It was only what John *thought*, not what he knew.

He wondered what to do. Then he decided that he, too, would hide at the edge of Oaktree Wood, just before the race, and he would see if anything happened. He could always give the alarm if an attack was made on number 62.

So, the next afternoon, feeling rather excited, John made his way to Oaktree Wood. He chose a tree that overlooked the stretch of road that ran by the wood, down which the runners would go, and he climbed it, making sure that there was nobody to see him.

Then he sat on a branch and waited. After a long time the first runner appeared. He was number 7. Apparently they were not running in their right order, but just anyhow, each starting off two minutes after the last.

Then number 16 appeared, and after him number 43. Then came 1 and 8 and 17, each some time after the other. Would 62 never come?

Then came one that looked like 62 but when he got nearer John saw that he was 63. Blow! Three or four more came – and then, surely, surely this was 62?

It was! He was a weedy youth, not a very good runner, with thin shoulders and skinny legs. He came along the road to a curve. And then things happened.

Somebody shot out from the hedge, clamped strong arms round Laurie and dragged him swiftly back into the undergrowth. His hand was over Laurie's mouth. John gasped. It was all so sudden. He caught a glimpse of a second man, and then Laurie was bundled away so quickly that except for a swishing of branches as the men forced their way into the undergrowth, there was nothing to be seen or heard.

John shinned down the tree quickly. He ran after the men, but they had disappeared. Then, in the distance, he heard the sound of a car being started up. Oh, so the men had a car hidden somewhere in a glade, had they? If only he could see it and take its number!

But by the time he got to the little clearing, the car was moving away, and all that John could see was that it was red. Red! Then probably it was the same car he had seen the man in the day before. He had got the two first letters and the last number of the car, but that was all. Blow!

The car came to a road in the wood and soon the sound of its engine died away in the distance. John sat down on an old tree trunk to think. Now he wished he had gone to the police, and reported what he had thought might happen. It *had* happened. He didn't know why, or what the men were after – but the thing was, Laurie Baxter had been attacked and taken away in a car. He'd better go to the police and tell them about that!

So off he went. He marched into the station and asked to speak to the sergeant, who was a friend of his uncle's. Then he told him what he knew.

'Please, sir, Laurie Baxter, number 62 in the Marathon, was attacked and taken off in a car, just as he was running beside Oaktree Wood,' said John. 'I saw it happen. I was up in a tree, waiting for it to happen, as a matter of fact.'

'*Waiting* for it to happen!' said the sergeant, surprised. 'What do you mean? How did you know it would happen?'

John told him everything – how he had overheard the number 62 in the wood, said by the man from the car – how he had examined all houses that might be the 62 meant – and then how he had thought it must be the number 62 of the Marathon runners.

'And it was,' said John. 'I wonder why Laurie Baxter was attacked, though.'

'I don't,' said the sergeant, grimly. 'I have an idea that he was in a burglary committed three weeks ago, and that he got off with most of the goods and sold them – whilst the others got nothing! They were scared in the middle of the robbery, and two of them fled, but Laurie apparently didn't. He waited, then when all was quiet, he took the goods and made off. I reckon the other fellows are angry with him, and want to know what he's done with their share!'

'Oh,' said John. 'But why didn't you arrest Laurie then, if you knew all this?'

'We questioned him, and put a watch on him,' said the sergeant, 'but we thought if we let him go free the others might make contact with him – and then we'd pull in the whole lot. But now it looks as if we've lost them all.'

'Well, sir – I managed to get the first two letters and the last number of their car,' said John, eagerly. 'Look – ST . . o. The car was red, sir, and was a sports saloon.'

'Good work!' said the sergeant, and took John's notebook. 'This will help tremendously. We can stop all cars of this description.'

Then a radio call at once went out to police patrols. 'Calling all cars, calling all cars. Please watch for a red car, make unknown, sports saloon type, first two letters ST, last number o. Three men inside. Hold for questioning. Over.'

'Can I stay here and see if anything happens, please?' asked John, excited.

'Right,' said the sergeant. 'Seeing that you've brought us so much information, you can wait – I might want to ask you more questions, mightn't I?'

So John waited. He had a cup of tea with the sergeant and felt very important. Many telephone calls came in, but nothing exciting, until at last there came the one the sergeant wanted. He turned to John.

'They've got them! The car was caught at Reading. The whole number is STA 120. It's a Humber, sports saloon, red. Three men inside, one of them Laurie Baxter. *Now* we'll get going!'

They did. Laurie was so angry with his companions for attacking and kidnapping him that he gave the whole show away. He told where the rest of the unsold stolen goods were, and related his companions' share in the various robberies they had committed together.

'So now,' finished the sergeant, smiling at the excited boy in front of him, 'they'll all spend a nice quiet little time thinking over their sins in prison. They'll commit no more robberies for a while – thanks to you, Detective John!'

And Detective John went proudly home. He'd solved another problem. Now – what would the next one be?

6. The Secret of Sky-Top Hill

'Where shall we go today?' said John. 'It's freezing. We'd better go for a sharp walk.'

'Well, let's show Harry the old ruin,' said Molly. 'The one at the bottom of Sky-Top Hill.'

Their cousin Harry looked at Molly. 'What a lovely name for a hill! And what's this old ruin? Let's go!'

'Come on, then,' said John, pulling on his coat. 'Look, you can see Sky-Top Hill from here – that steep hill sticking up into the sky. It's so wild and steep that nobody ever goes there. The old ruin is near the bottom of it. It was once an inn.'

They set off, walking sharply in the frosty air. It took them nearly an hour to reach the old inn, which was indeed nothing but a ruin now.

'People say that smugglers used to run this inn,' said Molly, climbing over a tumbledown bit of wall. 'It's terribly old – don't you think it *feels* old?'

It did. All the children thought it had a strange feeling. They wandered about in the ruined building, which had most of its roof off now

except for one piece over what had been the big
old kitchen.

'Once we played keeping house here,' said
Molly. 'We even made a fire in that old fire-
place, and we kept bread and potted meat in the
larder. It was fun!'

'Let's light a fire today and keep ourselves
warm!' said Harry. 'I'll go and get some dead
twigs and bits of wood.'

But the fire wouldn't burn. John dragged out
the twigs and put his head into the grate, looking
up the chimney to see if anything had fallen
down to block it.

'Sometimes birds build their nests at the top,
and the bits fall down and stop up the chimney,'
he said.

'But it's such an *enormous* old chimney!' said
Harry. 'Surely no bird's nest could stop it up!'

'Well – there *is* something blocking it,' said
John. 'A few bricks have fallen in or something.
Wait – I'll poke my stick up and see if I can move
them.'

He poked up his walking-stick. The bricks
were lodged very loosely across the chimney, and
they fell down into the grate with a clatter and a
cloud of dust, making the children jump. When
the dust had settled John put his head up again to
see if the chimney was clear.

'Hey – there's a big space where those bricks

fell from,' he called to the others. 'And I believe I can see something there. Got a torch, Harry?'

'Here you are,' said Harry and handed John a small torch. John shone it into the empty space.

'It's a box!' he said, excitedly. 'Hidden up the chimney! I wonder what's in it?'

'Treasure!' said Harry and Molly together. 'Quick, get it down and we'll see!'

John managed to get down the box. It was of some kind of metal, but it felt fairly light. The children put it on the window-sill, and looked at it. It was locked.

'We must smash it open!' said John. 'Hey – what a find! I bet there's some kind of secret inside!'

'What shall we smash the box with?' said Harry, red with excitement. 'Isn't it old and rusty? Whatever was it hidden up the chimney for?'

'There's an old broken poker somewhere,' said Molly, looking round. 'Yes, there it is. John, smash the box with that.'

Crash! The poker came down on the box. The rusty lock gave way, and the lid hung loose. John opened it.

Inside was a roll of thick yellowed paper. John picked it out of the box and smoothed it flat. There was nothing else in the box at all.

'Just an old paper!' he said in disappointment. The others bent over it.

'It's a rough kind of map!' said Harry. 'Look – there are the points of the compass shown in that corner – north, south, east, and west. And here's what looks like a road – it seems to fork here and there – but one piece is marked very thick in black ink. That road must lead somewhere.'

'Yes – but what road is it?' asked Molly. 'It's got no name!'

'Here's something written in this corner,' said John. 'It's very faded. Wait a bit – Y-e-w-t-r-e-e – that's what it looks like. The road seems to start from there.'

'Yew-tree!' said Molly. 'Well, this was called Yew-tree Inn, wasn't it? But there's no road at all from here except back to Lanning Village, where we've just come from. Why should anyone make a map of that, and hide it?'

'It's not that road, silly,' said John. 'We know it doesn't wind like this, and fork here and there – and anyway on this map the road shown runs in the opposite direction.'

'It's strange,' said Harry, looking through the window to the north, where the road or path on the map was supposed to run. 'There's not even a footpath there.'

'Hang on – there used to be an enormous old tree, a yew, growing at the corner of the inn!' said

Molly, suddenly. 'It's gone now – but the stump is still there. It grew out of the corner of the stable. I remember Daddy telling me about it.'

'Let's go and look,' said John. So out of the old kitchen they went, and into the tumbledown stable. Broken mangers were still on the wall. The floor was cobbled. A great heap of straw lay in one corner, flattened and brown.

'Here's the stump of the yew,' said John, and he pointed to a rotting stump at one end. 'Look, they had to make the wall bend in just here, so as not to spoil the tree.'

The stump was by the old heap of straw. John kicked some of the straw away – and then saw something odd!

'Hey! Look! The floor isn't cobbled here! There's a wooden trap-door. Do you suppose the road marked on that old map goes underground – a smuggler's way to somewhere?'

'Heave up the trap-door!' cried Harry. 'We'll soon see!'

The trap-door had an iron handle let into it. John tried to pull it to open the trap-door, but it would not budge.

'I've got a rope,' said Harry, who always carried extraordinary things about with him, just in *case* they were needed. He undid a rope from round his waist. He slipped it double through the iron ring. Then the three children could pull on it together.

'Now – heave ho!' yelled Harry, and they pulled hard. The trap-door came up so suddenly that all three of them sat down hard, and lost their breath.

John was up first. He peered down into the space uncovered by the trap-door. 'Steps down!' he cried. 'Stone steps. I bet this is the entrance to the secret way marked on that map. It runs north on the map, doesn't it – well, that means we go right into Sky-Top Hill!'

It certainly looked as if it did. The steep rocky slope of Sky-Top Hill rose up directly in front of them, and any underground path must lead into it. How strange!

'Shall we go down?' asked Molly, half afraid, as she peered down into the darkness. 'John, do you think it leads to a smuggler's hiding-place – caves or something – you know, where smugglers kept their goods?'

'Perhaps,' said John. 'Of *course* we're going down! But if you're afraid, Molly, don't come.'

'I'm as brave as you!' said Molly, crossly. 'Of course I'm coming.'

One by one they went down the stone steps. It was a good thing Harry had a torch. There were twelve steps and then a tunnel, dark, narrow and low in places.

'This is the way marked on the map all right!' said John, in excitement.

'Shine your torch here, Harry – I want to have a look at the map and make sure I know the right direction. We don't want to go wandering off into any of the wrong forks.'

'I hope we don't get lost!' said Molly, suddenly feeling afraid. 'Harry, have you got some white chalk? You've usually got your pockets full of everything. We could make white crosses on the wall of the tunnel as we go, then if we miss our way we shall be able to find it again by following our chalk marks back to the stable!'

'Good idea!' said Harry, and fished a piece of chalk from his pocket. Then on they went again along the tunnel, Harry marking bold white crosses every now and then.

The passage opened out widely after a bit, and here and there other ways ran from it into the hill.

'It's absolutely honeycombed with tunnels!' said John. 'Natural ones too – not hacked out by men. This one looks as if it'll lead right to the very heart of the hill! Hey – isn't this an adventure!'

The three children groped their way along the passage by the light of Harry's torch. Sometimes the air smelt horrid. Harry kept on marking the wall with his white crosses as he went, and the children were glad to think they would be able to find their way safely back again if they were lost.

The passage kept more or less level. John stopped and looked at the map whenever they came to a fork, so that he would know which one to take, the one going to the right or to the left.

'We must be getting very deep underground,' he said. 'The hill must be rising over us very high now. We shall soon come under its top!'

'I bet that's where we shall find something,' said Harry, marking another chalk cross. 'I bet that's where the old-time smugglers hid their goods!'

'We may find some!' said Molly, excited. 'Oh, do come on!'

Suddenly they came into a place that seemed at first to be a great cave – but daylight shone down into it! The children looked round and then up in amazement.

'Why – we're in a sort of deep, deep pit – and that's daylight shining in from the top. There's a hole in the top of Sky-Top Hill, and it drops right down to where we stand!'

They were quite right. There was an odd opening in the top of Sky-Top Hill, a shaft that went right down to the heart of it, ending where the children stood.

And in the caves round about were many strange things! 'Boxes!' said Molly. 'Crates!

They look ancient. I'm sure the smugglers hid their things here.'

'Hey, look over there!' said John, suddenly, and he pointed to the ground. 'A cigarette end – and an empty cigarette packet! Now who in the world can have left these here?'

It did seem odd to see the cigarette end and packet lying there among all the old-time boxes and crates.

'Who comes here – and why?' said Harry, suddenly dropping his voice to a whisper.

But before the others could answer, they heard something that made them jump violently. They heard a man's whistle – someone whistling a dance tune!

'There's someone coming!' said John, in a low tone. 'Look – from out of that cave over there. Hide, quick! We'll watch what he does!'

The children crouched behind a big empty crate in the darkness of an overhanging rock. They waited, their hearts beating loudly.

A figure came into sight. A broad young man, kicking a stone in front of him as if he were bored. He sat down on a box.

The children didn't make a sound. Somehow they felt the man wouldn't be at all pleased to know that they were there. They were afraid.

'He can't be up to any good,' thought John.

'We'd better try and find out what he's doing here!'

The children crouched silently behind the big box, keeping their eyes on the man. After a while he left his place and climbed a little way up the side of the pit, where a great rock made a kind of shelf.

Here he tinkered about with something, for the children could hear metallic sounds. There was evidently some kind of machinery up there.

'Molly! Harry! I bet that man's a smuggler, diamonds or gold or something!' said John, in a whisper. 'If I get a chance I'm going up on to that ledge to see what he's got there. I can't imagine what it is. If I get caught you must both go back down the secret passage and tell about this, and get help. See?'

'Oh John – don't,' said Molly, scared. 'Don't climb up to that ledge.'

'Sh!' said John, as the man climbed down again. He disappeared into a cave. 'Now's my chance!' said John, and darted out from his hiding-place. He climbed quickly to the ledge and stared in surprise. A strange kind of lantern or lamp was there, its face tilted upwards to the sky far above.

'What's it for?' wondered John – and then he heard a warning whistle from Harry. The man was coming again. John tried to scramble down.

But he was too late! The man saw him, made a dart at him and caught him. He shook him so fiercely that poor John thought his teeth would fall out.

'What are you doing here? You'll be sorry for yourself soon!' said the man, and flung John into a small cave. He fixed a great crate in front of it. 'You'll see what happens to nasty little boys who spy around! Have you done anything to that lamp up there?'

The man climbed up to see. Harry ran to free John but there was no time. 'Go for help, idiot!' said John. 'Quick, before he sees you.'

The others fled into the secret passage without being seen. How glad they were to think that they had the white chalk marks to follow!

John was left behind. The day went slowly by. He was hungry and thirsty but the man gave him nothing to eat or drink.

And then at night, when it was quite dark, a strange and powerful glow gradually filled the shaft, coming into the cave where John was a prisoner. And, at the same time, there came the drone of an aeroplane engine overhead!

'That glow is from the lamp on the ledge half-way down the pit!' said John, to himself, filled with excitement. 'It can only be seen by anyone flying directly overhead. It's a signal of some sort. What a clever idea – yes, that man is signalling with the lamp – the light keeps going on and off!'

The engine droned overhead for a little while. John heard a loud thud and then the aeroplane made off and the strange glow died away.

Darkness came again, and poor John trembled in his damp prison. If only the others would come.

What had happened to the other two? They had hurried away down the dark secret passage by the light of Harry's torch. Harry held the torch and Molly followed close at his heels.

And then they suddenly lost their way! They took the wrong fork, and then they tried to make their way back, they found they were lost. 'I thought we were following your chalk-marks on the wall!' said Molly, almost in tears. 'How did we miss the way?'

Both children were frightened. They sat down to have a rest and to work out which way to go. At last they set out again, and after a long time, to their great delight they came across Harry's chalk crosses on the wall!

'Now for goodness sake don't let's lose them again!' said Molly. 'It's getting so late – and I'm starving! It will be dark before we get home!'

It was almost dark when the two children staggered in at the garden door, and Molly called loudly for her mother. Very soon she had told her the extraordinary happenings of the day.

'I'll ring up the police,' said Mrs Johnson, who was astonished and worried. 'This is serious. We must certainly rescue poor John!'

Soon the police came in a big car, and off they all went to the old ruined inn. 'We had better get to the pit by way of the underground passage,' said the Inspector. 'Something funny is going on inside Sky-Top Hill!'

They all crept as silently as possible down the secret passage. When they came to the part that opened into the pit, they stopped in wonder – for a strange red glow lay all round. It was the glow cast by the powerful lamp hidden inside the hill. Its light shone up, and could be seen by the aeroplane which was even then droning overhead – but nothing could be seen of the glowing lamp by any watcher out in the countryside!

'Ingenious,' said the Inspector, under his breath. 'We've known for a long time that there's a diamond smuggling gang operating in this area, but we've never been able to catch them red-handed. Well, you children have done a good job of work for us today.'

Then the Inspector and his men took charge of affairs, and things began to happen! The man by the lamp was captured. Other men hidden in comfortable caves were routed out and arrested. A hoard of diamonds worth thousands of pounds was uncovered; the aeroplane had been coming once a week to drop its illegal cargo into Sky-Top Hill. It was a very clever idea.

'Nice little nest of smugglers,' said the Inspector grimly. 'Come along children – you've had enough excitement for one day!'

'What an exciting adventure!' said John happily, as he got into bed that night. 'I do wish someone would write and tell other children. I'm sure they'd like to hear about it!'

7. Case of the Five Dogs

One day, when John was sitting reading in his garden, he heard his name called. He looked up and saw the face of a little girl peeping over the wall.

'Hallo, Meg – what do you want?' asked John.

'Oh John – can we come in for a minute. There's Colin here and George, and me and Katie. We want to talk to you.'

'Come on over the wall then,' said John, surprised. They all clambered over. Meg and Katie were ten, George and Colin were about twelve. With them were their dogs.

'What's up?' asked John. 'Hey, keep your dogs in order, won't you? Dad's just planted out some new things in the beds.'

The children settled down on the grass, each holding the collar of their own dog. 'You see, John, we know you're a very good detective,' said George. 'So we thought you might help us. Something awful has happened.'

'What?' asked John, feeling rather important at being called a very good detective.

'This morning some of Farmer Warner's sheep

were chased by dogs,' said George. 'One fell in the stream and broke its leg.'

'And the farmer went to the police and he said it was *our* dogs that did it,' said Katie, almost in tears. 'He said one of his sheep was killed the other day by dogs, and he *saw* an Aberdeen like my Jock, a terrier like George's Sandy, a Sealyham like Meg's and a spaniel like Colin's in the road outside the field. So now he says it was our dogs that killed his sheep last week, and ours that chased them today.'

'And perhaps they'll be shot,' said Colin, gloomily. 'Or else our fathers will be fined. But we *know* it wasn't our dogs.'

'We want you to help us,' said George. 'You've got to prove that it was somebody else's dog, not ours, see? You're a clever enough detective for that, aren't you?'

'Well – I don't know,' said John. 'This isn't quite like any case I've had before. To begin with – *some* dog must have killed that sheep. If we could prove that first, we'd be halfway to saving *your* dogs. But we don't know what dog did it.'

'Yes, we do,' said Colin at once. 'It was Wilkins' dog – you know, the man who comes all round the district cleaning windows and doing odd jobs. He's got a horrible black dog, big and fierce and ugly.'

'Oh, yes, I know it,' said John. 'It's the only

dog I'm really scared of. It looks so fierce and it growls like anything if anyone goes near it. I always think it looks as bad-tempered as its master.'

'Yes, that's the one,' said Meg.

'But how do you know it's the dog that killed the sheep?' asked John. 'Did you see it?'

'No, but we know someone who did,' said George. 'You know, there's a gypsy caravan near that field, and there are some children living there. One's called Julie, and we sometimes speak to her. She told us she saw the big black dog chase the sheep and kill it.'

'Well then – that's easy! She's only got to tell the police that!' said John.

'She won't. She's afraid of the police. She says if we try to make her tell, she'll say she doesn't know anything,' said Colin. 'She says her father would beat her black and blue if she told anything to the police. They don't like policemen.'

'I told the policeman who came about my dog that I knew it was the big black one belonging to Wilkins,' said George. 'But when he came again he said Wilkins said he wasn't in the district that evening, so it couldn't have been his dog, because it never leaves him.'

'And now it's *our* dogs that are bearing the blame for everything!' said Meg, fiercely, putting her arms round her Sealyham. 'Why, Scamp doesn't even chase *cats*! I'm not going to have him shot for something that isn't his fault.'

'So you see, John, you *must* do something!' said Katie. 'We could only think of coming to you. Will you help us?'

'Yes, of course,' said John, who was very fond of dogs. 'But its going to be difficult to make a man own up to his dog killing a sheep, if he's already said that neither he nor his dog were here that evening. Have you asked if anyone else saw him or his dog that evening near Farmer Warner's sheep field?'

'Yes, we've asked *everyone*,' said Colin. 'But nobody did. You know, there was a big meeting on the green that night, and simply everyone was there. There might not have been a single person anywhere near the field when the sheep was killed – except Julie, and she won't tell.'

'She ought to tell,' said Meg. 'That dog once bit their baby. It's still got the scar. Julie showed it to me.'

'It's an awful dog,' said George. 'It'll end in killing somebody. John, can you do something?'

'Well, I'll try,' said John. 'But somehow I just don't know how to begin. First – what day was the sheep killed?'

'Last Friday,' said Colin. 'I was on the green with the others. We were listening to the speaker, and I was watching an aeroplane doing stunts in the sky. It wrote "Moon" against the blue, and we all laughed, because it was Mr Moon who was speaking at the meeting. It was a good advertisement for him. He wants everyone to vote for him, doesn't he?'

'Fancy hiring an aeroplane to write your name in the sky!' said Meg. 'I wish one would write mine. I'd feel very important.'

'Well, let's get back to our subject,' said John. 'The sheep was killed on Friday. Julie says she saw Wilkins' black dog kill it. Wilkins says he wasn't here and neither was his dog. Where does he say he was, I wonder?'

'He swears he was fifteen miles away,' said Colin. 'Out on his bicycle. He says he went to speak to a man at Five-Mile-Hill about some work, but the man wasn't there. Anyway, Wilkins swears he was miles and miles away from here. He says his dog loped along beside his bike all the way. So there you are!'

'Did Julie see Wilkins as well as his black dog, on Friday when the dog killed the sheep?' said John.

'No. But she said she heard his peculiar whistle, when he whistled to the dog to come to him,' said Colin. 'You know his whistle? It's awfully loud and shrill. He puts two fingers in his mouth when he does it. Julie can do it too. But I can't.'

'Well – it looks as if the dog *and* the man were there on Friday then, when everyone else was on the green listening to Mr Moon,' said John. 'But how in the world can we prove it?'

'Wilkins is coming again tomorrow,' said Meg, suddenly. 'It's his day for our village. Couldn't you talk to him, John?'

'Well . . .' said John, and stopped. He didn't like Wilkins, and he didn't think Wilkins would like him, either. And he certainly didn't like the man's dog. It gave him a horrid feeling when the big black creature sniffed round his ankles. He felt as if at any moment it might take a bite out of his leg. 'Oh, please, please do,' said Meg. 'We'll come and be with you, if you like. But we'd better leave our dogs at home, or that awful black dog will gobble them up!'

'Yes, for goodness sake don't bring your dogs,' said John, picturing a free fight between them and the black dog going on all round him. 'All right. I'll think of something to say to him. You can all be with me and listen to what he says.'

Wilkins always went to the village inn, when he was near, and brought out a drink for himself. He sat down on the log bench beside the green in the evening sunshine, and ate bread and jam and drank his beer. His dog always lay at his feet.

'He'll be there about six o'clock,' said John. 'I often see him there then. We'll be playing about, and I'll go up and try to draw him into conversation. You can all listen hard. But don't mention the word "dogs" or he'll be on his guard.'

'Right,' said Colin. 'He doesn't know any of us. Now mind, everybody – leave your dogs at home so that they can't get out.'

John was a bit worried about this new problem. It wasn't like his others at all. He didn't see how to tackle it, no matter how hard he puzzled about it. He lay in bed that night and pondered over it.

Julie had seen the dog killing the sheep and had heard Wilkins whistling to him that Friday evening. Therefore he must have been there. But he said he was miles and miles away. Everyone else, unfortunately, seemed to have been on the green, listening to Mr Moon, and looking at his name being written in the sky. It was fortunate for Wilkins that nobody was anywhere near Farmer Warner's field that evening!

After a long while John made a plan. He didn't think it was very good – but it just might work. He'd see.

So, the next evening, about six o'clock, he, Meg, Katie, Colin and George went to the green, near the Rose and Crown Inn. They began to play a game with a bat and ball. No dog was near. All had been left safely at home.

'Here's Wilkins now,' said John, in a low voice. 'See, there's his van, and that awful black dog is sitting up beside him just as he always does.'

The van drew up outside the inn. The man got out and went inside. He came out with a tankard and went to sit in the evening sunshine on a wooden bench beside the green. He pulled a packet of sandwiches out of his pocket.

'We'll give him a minute or two, then I'll go up and ask if he knows the time,' said John, and threw the ball to Colin. All the children kept an eye on the black dog. He lay beside his master, but they felt that at any moment he might go after their ball.

In a little while John went up to Wilkins, followed by the others. 'Could you please tell me the time?' he asked.

'Look at the church clock,' said Wilkins, in a surly voice. Blow! John had forgotten that the church clock could be seen from the green.

'Oh, yes, of course – thanks,' he said. 'A quarter past six,' he said to the others. Then he looked at the black dog.

'Fine big dog you've got,' he said, politely. 'I bet he eats a lot. Can he catch rabbits?'

Wilkins looked at him. 'My dog don't chase nothing,' he said. 'He don't chase even a sparrow. He just keeps alongside of me.'

'But surely he would chase a cat?' said Colin, joining in. 'All dogs chase cats.'

'Well, this one don't,' said Wilkins. 'He don't chase nothing.'

The dog looked at them out of bloodshot eyes and growled.

'He won't bite, will he?' said Meg, retreating hastily.

'Never bit anyone in his life,' said Wilkins. 'Best-tempered dog I ever had.'

The dog growled again and showed yellow teeth. None of the children liked him at all.

'Is he afraid of anything?' asked John. 'You know – afraid of guns or noises or anything like that? Some dogs are.'

'No. He ain't afraid of nothing,' said Wilkins.

'I knew a dog once that was scared stiff of aeroplanes,' said John.

'Mine don't mind nothing,' said Wilkins and took a long drink.

'I think I can hear an aeroplane now,' said John. 'Oh no – it's a car. Hey – have you heard of those aeroplanes that can write in the sky? I wish *I* could see one!'

'You did see one – don't you remember – it wrote MOON in the sky,' said Colin, astonished at John's forgetfulness.

'No – surely it wrote SUN,' said John. 'Wait a

bit – yes – I'm remembering – it wrote SUN, didn't it?'

'Gah – it wrote MOON, of course,' said Wilkins, munching hard. 'Can't you read, then? It wrote MOON plain as anything. That's a wonderful thing that is, to write in smoke in the sky.'

'Let's see – it was a white aeroplane, wasn't it?' said John, as if he was trying hard to remember. But everyone put him right.

'No, it was one of those silvery-grey ones, it was, really!'

John appealed to Wilkins. 'It wasn't, was it? It was white.'

'You're wrong,' said the man, and took another sandwich. 'It was grey. Saw it as clear as could be. *And* the markings too – L.G.O. they were, whatever they might mean. My eyes are as good as yourn any day.'

He got up, emptied the dregs from his tankard on to the grass and went into the inn. He came out again, followed by his dog, and got into his van. Without so much as a wave he drove off.

The children crowded round John. Only Colin had seen how his little plan had worked. The others hadn't.

'John – how very, very clever of you – to lead the conversation round to aeroplanes like that – and to make him say he'd seen that one writing

MOON in the sky, and to make him describe it too!'

'Well – but what's so clever about all that?' said Meg.

'Can't you see, silly? That plane came over on Friday evening, and *only* Friday evening – and Wilkins said he was miles away! Well, how could he have seen that aeroplane writing in the sky, if he wasn't here?'

There was silence. John and Colin looked triumphantly round. 'There you are!' said John. 'He's admitted he was here – and we've got five witnesses. Come on, we'll go to the police station.'

And off they all went. John's friend the sergeant was there, and he took them into his room, looking amused. He listened to their whole story without interrupting once. Then he made a few notes.

'Very interesting,' he said, 'very, very interesting. And very smart work too, Detective John. We will follow this up and ask Wilkins how he managed to see this aeroplane doing its tricks when he was fifteen miles away.'

The children next went to Julie. They told her what had happened. 'Suppose Wilkins admits he and his dog were here, will you say what you saw?' asked Colin. 'You must, you know – because you'll be a proper witness then.'

Julie looked scared. 'Will I get into trouble if I don't say?' she asked.

'Yes, awful trouble!' said John, hard-heartedly. 'Oh, Julie – surely you will speak up for our dogs – you wouldn't want them to be shot, would you, instead of a wicked dog that has killed a sheep and already bitten your baby?'

'Well, all right then,' said Julie. So when a policeman called, Julie told him all she had seen, and, armed with this, and the other information the children had given him, the sergeant went off to interview Wilkins.

He came back again in his car, and saw the children gathered together on the green, waiting for him. This time they had their dogs with them.

He stopped his car. The children crowded round him. 'Well, he's confessed,' said the sergeant. 'He *was* in the district, his dog *was* with him, it did go for the sheep, and then he whistled it off. He says he didn't know a sheep was killed at the time, and was too afraid to confess when he did hear. I don't know about that. Anyway, what do you think that dog did?'

'What?' asked the children. The sergeant showed them a bandaged leg.

'Took a nip out of *me*!' he said. 'Silly thing to do, wasn't it? He's going to be punished for all his misdeeds, you may be sure – and your dogs can

now go home without a stain on their character –
thanks to good old Detective John!'

'Woof,' said the dogs at once. 'Woof!' And
they tried to lick John as if they actually understood what he had done for them. He really is a
very good detective, isn't he?

8. The Lonely Old House

Harry, Cathy and Dick had come to stay at their little seaside cottage, not far from Kelty Cliffs. They loved it, because it was so near the cliff-path that led down to the beach, and had such a glorious view of the sea.

This was the third year they had come there, but this time Mother and Daddy hadn't come. They had gone to Ireland to see Mother's sister, who was ill. So Miss Truman, their mother's friend, had come to be with them in the cottage.

'I like Miss Truman, but she doesn't really seem to listen to anything we say,' complained Cathy. 'She's so busy with the cooking and the shopping and the mending that she just says, "Yes, dear, really," or "No, dear, really," all the time.'

'Well, never mind,' said Harry. 'It suits *me*! We can do just what we like. Miss Truman never seems to mind anything. Anyway, it's gorgeous here.'

So it was. The weather was fine and hot, the bathing was good, they had a very old boat of their own, and there were lovely walks all round.

There were no houses near them at all except

one. This was a big old house set in tall trees not very far away. Each year it had been empty, and the children now took no notice of it at all. It just stood there, silent and gloomy, with no one going up the drive or down.

And then one day something happened that made the children suddenly take an interest in the old empty house. They went with Kim, their Airedale, for a walk. They passed near the empty house, set round with high walls. Then Kim suddenly darted off, barking.

'A rabbit,' said Harry. 'Poor old Kim. He never will learn that rabbits won't wait for him. Hi, Kim! Come here.'

But Kim didn't come, and from his excited barking the children imagined that he really did have hopes of a rabbit. They walked on a little way, and then whistled Kim again.

'Blow him!' said Harry. 'Now we'll have to go and drag him backwards out of a rabbit-hole. One of these days he really will get stuck halfway down.'

They went to look for Kim, and then suddenly they came on something they had never seen before. It was an odd little tumbledown house made of the white stone of the district. It stood there among the trees, covered with ivy and moss, its roof gone, and its one window without glass.

'What a funny little place,' said Harry, going up to it. 'Whatever was it built here for?'

'This wood once belonged to that old empty house,' said Cathy. 'Mother told me so. I expect it was a summer-house or something, built for the people who used to live there long ago.'

'Kim's inside!' said Dick. 'He must have chased a rabbit there. Kim, come here.'

But Kim was very busy scraping hard at the floor of the little stone house. The rabbit had run into the house and disappeared. Therefore it must still be there, and Kim meant to scrape up the whole floor rather than lose it! He was a very persistent dog.

He had scraped away the moss and earth from part of the floor. Dick went up to take hold of his collar, and then stopped in surprise. Kim had scraped away quite a hole – and at the bottom of it was a flat stone – and in the stone was an iron handle!

'Look – that's a bit funny,' said Dick, pointing it out to the others. 'See? Kim's scraped away the earth and come to the stone floor – and there's an iron handle in that particular stone flag. I wonder why?'

'Ooooh – how strange,' said Cathy at once. 'Usually stones with iron handles in them are meant to be lifted up – like trap-doors. Oh,

Harry, don't let's go for a walk – let's dig down and explore a bit.'

'No. We shan't find anything, and shall get ourselves dirty and tired out,' said Harry. 'There's probably nothing in it at all. Come on.'

'Oh no, Harry – do let's just scrape away all the earth and see if there *is* anything exciting,' begged Dick. 'I've read loads of adventure stories, but I've never had an adventure myself. This might lead to one.'

'Don't be silly,' said Harry. He was thirteen, and thought the twelve-year-old Dick rather babyish. 'Come on, Kim.'

'Well, you go for a walk alone!' called Cathy, crossly. 'I shall stay with Dick – and maybe we *shall* have an adventure – and we'll jolly well have it without you!'

Harry snorted, and, with Kim at his heels, he went on by himself. Silly kids! Let them stay and make themselves into a mess if they wanted to.

Cathy and Dick stared down at the stone, with its iron handle. 'Shall we go back and get our spades?' said Cathy, eagerly. 'We can't do it with our hands.'

'Yes, let's,' said Dick. 'And we'll bring a torch too.'

'What for?' asked Cathy.

'Well – you never know,' said Dick. 'It's a very

good thing to have about you, if you're expecting an adventure.'

They soon got their spades and went back again to the strange little stone house. What a tumbledown place it was! People could not have been into it for years and years.

They began to dig away the earth and moss from the floor of the house. They cleared it all from the stone flag beneath, and then saw that it was indeed meant to be lifted, for it distinctly moved a little when both children tugged at it!

'Isn't this exciting!' said Dick, pushing his hair back from his dripping forehead, and smearing his face with black dirt. 'Come on, let's use all our strength and see if it'll budge.' Dick and Cathy pulled with all their might, panting and groaning with their efforts.

Nothing happened. They sat down to get their breath. 'Let's run our spades all round the edges of the flagstone. It's stuck fast with soil, I expect,' said Dick. 'If we loosen that away, the stone might come up more easily.'

So they dug their spades all round the edges of the stone, and cleared out the dirt. Then they took hold of the iron handle and tried again. And, quite suddenly, the stone moved! It first moved upwards, and then slid sideways and downwards in a peculiar way. It left a hole, dark and mysterious.

'Gracious!' said Cathy, speaking in a whisper, though she didn't quite know why. 'Look at that!'

Dick took out his torch. He flashed it down the hole. 'Steps!' he said. 'Look - stone steps - awfully steep and narrow, though. Hey, Cathy - isn't this exciting? Shall we go down?'

'No,' said Cathy, half afraid.

'Well - *I'm* going, anyway,' said Dick, and he put his foot down to the first step.

'I won't let you go alone,' said Cathy. 'If you're going, I'm coming with you. Oh dear - I wish Harry was here.'

'Well, *I* don't,' said Dick. 'He wouldn't stay and help so he doesn't deserve to share in this adventure!'

He went down to the next step. Then to the next. There appeared to be a missing or broken one after that and Dick missed his footing and fell. He gave a yell and Cathy jumped in fright.

But Dick hadn't far to fall - only two or three more steps. He landed on some soft earth, afraid that he might break his torch. But luckily he didn't.

'It's all right,' he shouted up. 'There's a step missing, so look out. I'll shine my torch for you.'

Cathy got down without falling. Dick flashed his torch round. A narrow dark passage ran downwards at the end of the steps.

'It looks horrible,' said Cathy, with a shiver. 'Wherever does it go to?'

'Goodness knows,' said Dick. 'Come on. Let's find out.'

'We shan't meet anything awful, shall we?' asked Cathy, nervously, not quite knowing what she expected to meet.

'Well, we might see a worm or two,' said Dick, cheerfully. 'Do come on. Can't you *enjoy* an adventure, Cathy? Or are you scared of everything?'

'I'm not scared,' said Cathy, in a brave tone. 'Only – I'd like you to go first, Dick.'

Dick had every intention of going first. Down the narrow, sloping passage he went, with Cathy close behind him. It smelt musty and damp. Dick suddenly wondered if the air was good. He had read somewhere that if the air underground was not good, explorers fell down in a kind of stupor, and died. Still, he felt quite all right, so maybe the air was good.

The passage stopped sloping downwards and went along on the level. It no longer wound about but ran practically straight. Dick tried to puzzle out what direction it could be running in – towards the sea, perhaps? But he could not make up his mind.

He kept the torch pointed towards the ground so as to see where to tread. He did not realize that the roof of the passage suddenly sloped low, and he got a terrific bang on the head as he walked into it. He stopped suddenly with a cry, and Cathy bumped into him.

'Oh! What's the matter?'

'Look out for the roof – it gets low here,' said Dick, and bent his head down to walk under the low part. Soon he came to a full-stop. His torch showed him more stone steps – this time going upwards.

Up them went Dick, followed by Cathy, who was now wishing to goodness they could see day-light again. They came out into a great wide dark place, and could not imagine where they were.

'It's a cellar!' said Cathy, suddenly. 'Look, there are old cobwebby bottles over there. Oooh – look at that enormous spider. Dick, don't let it come over here.'

'It won't,' said Dick. 'It's much more scared of you than you are of it! Yes, you're right. We're in a cellar – and if I'm not mistaken, it's the cellar of the old empty house!'

'Do you really think so?' said Cathy, aston-ished. 'How can we get out then?'

'Up the cellar steps to the kitchen, I should think,' said Dick, and began to flash his torch here and there to try and find out where any more steps were. He soon found them, in a distant corner. This time they were made of wood, not stone. The two children went up them, to a door at the top. It was shut.

Dick turned the handle. It opened into a great kitchen, with a huge range at one end for cooking.

'Yes, it *is* the old house,' said Dick. 'Hey – what fun! We can come here and play. We'll explore it from top to bottom.'

'Will it matter if we do?' said Cathy. 'Won't anybody mind?'

'Why should they?' said Dick. 'We shan't do any harm or damage. Hey, it's good to see a bit of daylight, isn't it, even if it has to come through such dirty windows!'

It *was* good to see daylight. A few rays of sunshine straggled through the window nearby, and lay on the floor. It was these that showed Dick something which astonished him. He gave an exclamation.

'Look there! Footprints in the dust on the floor! They're not ours, they're too big. I wonder who comes here.'

Cathy stared at them fearfully. They looked freshly made. She didn't like them. Suppose there was somebody in the house now?

'Let's go back,' she whispered. 'Somebody might catch us. I don't like it.'

Dick was beginning to feel he didn't much like it either. It was strange to be in an old, old empty house – and see fresh footprints in the dust on the floor. The house was so quiet too – as if it was listening for something. Dick clutched Cathy and made her jump.

'Come on. We'll go back. We've seen enough. We'll come back with Harry sometime.'

They hurried to the cellar door, and down the wooden steps. They found their way to the hole where the other stone steps began and went down those into the dark passage. And then somebody jumped out at them from the passage with a yell that almost frightened the life out of them.

The somebody clutched hold of them tightly and yelled again. Then Dick struck out crossly and yelled back. 'It's you, Harry. You scared us! You really are horrible.'

Harry laughed. He was very, very glad to find the others. He and Kim had come back to the little stone house and discovered the hole where the stone had been, and the steps leading down. Cross to think that Dick and Cathy had actually discovered something exciting, Harry had gone down after them.

But he had no torch and it was not at all pleasant groping about in the darkness. He longed to hear the cheerful voices of the others – and at last he did hear them! He had waited to jump out at Dick, and had given both Dick and Cathy a terrible fright.

'Sorry,' said Harry. 'Did I really scare you? Get down, Kim. Dick, where does this lead to? You found an adventure after all!'

'You bet!' said Dick. 'One up on you, old boy! Gosh, I'm glad you're here, Harry, even though you did scare me stiff. Do you know, this passage leads to the cellar of the old empty house? And we've been up into the kitchen – and there are fresh footprints there in the dust of the floor!'

'Whew!' said Harry. 'That's funny. Who comes here then? Perhaps it's just some tramp at night.'

'But we *know* the place is locked and barred,' said Dick, 'because we've often tried to get into it ourselves from the outside, just to see what it was like. And we never could. It can't be just a tramp!'

'Let's go back again and I'll have a look,' said Harry. So back they went and, once they were in the kitchen, Harry saw the big footprints too.

'Yes – they're freshly-made all right,' he said. 'My word – listen – there's somebody opening the front door! Quick, down to the cellar!'

Their hearts beating fast, the children made for the cellar door. They stood there and listened for a moment. They heard the front door open, and then to their great amazement they heard a voice they knew well! It was old Mrs Harriman, who went out doing housework, and who came to them every Saturday, to help Miss Truman. Whatever was *she* doing here?

Kim whined, for he too recognized Mrs Harriman's voice, but Harry's hand tightened on his collar. No, he must not give them away. Mrs Harriman was talking to somebody.

'Well, here we are, Liza, and I must say it's a dreadful place, enough to give you the creeps. Fancy somebody coming along to live in it after all this time. Well, you and me's got our work cut out to clean the place up a bit, and scrub them filthy floors.'

Kim whined again, and the children retreated down the cellar.

'Funny,' came Mrs Harriman's booming voice, as she entered the great kitchen. 'I thought I heard a dog whining then. Shows you what your imagination can do!'

Harry softly shut the cellar door and went down the steps after the others. They made their way to the hole and went down the steps there into the passage. Soon they had arrived inside the little tumble-down stone house, glad to see the sunshine coming through the trees.

'Well – it wasn't so mysterious after all – seeing those footprints!' said Harry. 'They must have been made by somebody who came to look at the house. Fancy people coming to live here after all those years! I wonder who they are. Perhaps Mrs Harriman will know.'

'Don't tell her about the underground way into the house,' said Cathy. 'Let's make it our secret. I like secrets like that.'

'Course we won't tell her,' said Dick. 'Let's shut down the stone door, and pull bracken over it to hide it. It might be fun to use it again before the people come in.'

They went home with Kim, who looked very disappointed. He had hoped to find plenty of rabbits down that wonderful dark rabbit-hole – and there hadn't even been a smell of one!

Miss Truman did not seem to mind their coming home so dirty. She did not even ask where they had been. So long as they were in good health and hadn't hurt themselves she didn't really bother much about their escapades.

The next day was Saturday, so the children asked Mrs Harriman, when she came to do some scrubbing, if anyone was coming to the old house.

'Yes, there is,' said Mrs Harriman, settling herself down on the floor with a large pail of water and an outsize scrubbing-brush. 'My, my, look at this floor! Doesn't *anyone* wipe their feet in this house?'

'Only Kim,' said Cathy, with a giggle. 'Who's coming to the old, empty house, Mrs Harriman?'

'Well, that I don't rightly know,' said Mrs

Harriman, beginning to scrub vigorously. 'Mind your feet, Cathy. The house agent, he called on me, gave me the key, and said I was to go up and clean, with Liza. All he said was that a gentleman was coming to live there, a real recluse, he called him, though what that is I *don't* know.'

'Nor do I,' said Cathy. But the boys knew.

'It's somebody who wants to live away from everyone and not be bothered by visitors or anything,' said Dick. 'Well, he won't be bothered much there! When's he coming?'

'Next week, so I hear,' said Mrs Harriman. 'Mind your feet again, Cathy. And if anybody treads on where I've just scrubbed they won't get any of my chocolate buns for tea, and I tell you that straight.'

Everyone immediately went away from the gleaming wet part that Mrs Harriman had scrubbed. There didn't seem to be much more information they could get out of the char-woman, so they retired to the garden, where they picked and ate a large amount of purple plums.

'We could watch each day and see who comes,' said Dick. 'We can see the furniture vans. They will have to pass our cottage.'

'So they will,' said Cathy. So each day the children watched and on the next Wednesday they were rewarded by seeing two great vans come lumbering by. They followed the vans up to the old house.

Mrs Harriman was there with a paper in her hand, directing proceedings. 'All furniture marked D is to go into the dining-room,' she told the foreman. 'I'll show you which it is. And all marked K is to . . .'

'It's just the furniture – not the recluse man,' said Cathy, disappointed. 'Blow! We shan't see him now.'

The children were not interested in the furniture, so they went away. They found their bathing things and went to bathe. They then took out their leaky old boat, got caught in a current, and had to row so very hard back to shore that they were absolutely tired out.

They crawled back to their cottage, groaning and stiff. 'Done too much, I suppose?' said Miss Truman. 'Well, I'll get you some supper and then off to bed you must go. You'll be asleep in two shakes of a duck's tail, I should think.'

The boys were, but Cathy was too tired even to go to sleep! She tossed and turned. She heard the church clock down in the distant village strike ten, eleven and even twelve. She dozed a little and then heard it strike one.

And just as it had struck, she heard another noise. It was a car coming slowly and quietly along the lane by their cottage! Cathy was most surprised. No cars ever came along there, for the lane was a blind one, going only to their cottage and then a little distance on to the old empty house. Was the car going to stop at the cottage?

No, it was not. It went straight on past it, up the lane. Cathy listened. How very odd! Was it going to the old house? But how late at night to arrive!

She lay down again. The car did not come back. She listened for it for some time and then quite suddenly fell asleep.

In the morning she was not quite sure if she had dreamt it. So before she told the boys she went into the sandy lane and had a look round. Yes – there were the marks of the tyres. So she hadn't dreamt it.

'The recluse man has arrived at the old house,' Cathy announced at breakfast.

'How do you know?' said Harry, disbelievingly.

'Because I heard his car going by last night at about one o'clock,' said Cathy.

'That's morning, not night,' said Dick.

'Well, it was one o'clock in the morning, in the middle of the night,' said Cathy. 'And there are tyre marks in our lane this morning.'

The children went for a walk up to the old house after breakfast to see if they could see any sign of the 'recluse man' as Cathy would keep calling him. But the great iron gates were not only closed, but padlocked, and, as there were high walls all round the grounds, the children knew there was no way of getting in at all. Except, of course, by the underground passage!

'But we can't possibly use that again,' said Harry. 'Not now the house is occupied. It didn't matter when it was empty. My word, the recluse, whoever he is, means to keep everyone away, doesn't he!'

'What about food and milk and stuff?' wondered Cathy.

'Oh, he's probably got good stores,' said Harry. 'Come on – let's go and lie on the sand. I'm so stiff with rowing yesterday that I don't even want to bathe today!'

So, with Kim bounding along beside them, the children went down to the beach and forgot all about the strange old house. They spent a happy, lazy day together, and went off to bed, yawning, at nine o'clock.

Cathy had tossed and turned for hours the night before, so tonight she fell asleep at once. Dick did too, but Harry lay wide awake, listening to the owls hooting in the woods round the old lonely house. He was glad he was in his cosy cottage, not imprisoned in that great house, surrounded by high walls and tall trees.

He lay so that he could look out of the window.

It was very dark outside for the sky was clouded over, and there was no moon at all. He faced in the direction of the old house, which was a good way away, hidden by trees.

Harry lay there, gazing out for a little while – then he became conscious of some far-off light somewhere. Was it a light? He tried to focus his eyes in the direction from which he thought it came, and waited. Yes, it *was* some kind of light – faint and far off – and coming in flashes. How strange. Where did it come from?

He thought for a minute. It *could* come from the top windows of the old house. He could see those indistinctly through the tops of the trees in the daytime, if he looked out of his window. But why should a light come and go from there in the middle of the night?

He decided to get up and investigate. He pulled on shorts and jersey and went out, Kim running beside him, surprised and pleased to have a night-walk.

Harry made his way towards the old house. He could not see it in the dark, and almost bumped into the trunks of trees as he made his way between them.

And then he saw the light quite distinctly. It came from the topmost window of the old house, a pin-prick of light, flashing off and on, off and on, as if the owner was trying to signal to somebody. But to whom would anyone want to signal at night, in that lonely place? Nobody would ever see that pin-point of light, except by accident.

Then the light became fainter, and finally the flashes stopped altogether. Harry made a note of exactly where the window would be, and made up his mind to look for it the next day. Then back he went to bed, and fell asleep.

He told the others the next morning and they felt most excited. 'It's a mystery,' said Dick. 'There really is some mystery. We must solve it!'

They went to have a look at the window. It was the topmost one on the eastern side of the house – and it was barred.

'Well, that's nothing. It's always been barred, as long as we can remember,' said Dick. 'It was once a nursery, Mrs Harriman said.'

'Do you think there is anyone there now?' said Cathy. 'I mean – somebody we could see, if we climbed a tree, say?'

'Cathy, that's an *awfully* good idea!' said Harry at once. 'If I climb this tall tree here, its top will be about level with that window. I'll do it.'

The tree was a chestnut, and grew just outside the wall that ran round the grounds of the old house. Harry climbed it easily. He went steadily to the top and then slid out on a broad branch to get as near as he could to the barred window. But he was still so far away that he could not possibly see inside.

And then, just as he was going to get down, somebody came to the window and looked out. Harry expected to see an old man – but instead he saw a young boy with a shock of dark hair, enormous dark eyes and a pale face. He was most surprised, and stared across at the window in astonishment.

Harry gave one of his piercing whistles to get the boy's attention. The boy heard it and looked out. He suddenly saw Harry on the branch of the chestnut tree and was so amazed that he could only stand and stare. Harry yelled to him.

'Who are you?'

The boy put his finger to his lips and looked thoroughly scared. Harry did not shout again. Then the boy made a sign to Harry to wait, and disappeared from the window. He was away for a minute or two, then came back.

He put his finger to his lips again, to tell Harry not to make a noise. Then he began to hold up sheets of white notepaper, on each of which he had printed in bold black letters, one letter of the alphabet. He held them up one after another for Harry to see.

Harry jotted them down in his notebook as the boy held them up. 'I-A-M-A-P-R-I-S-O-N-E-R.' It was not until he had got them all jotted down that Harry suddenly saw what words they spelt. 'I am a prisoner!'

Gosh! thought Harry. So that's what the light meant last night. He was signalling with his torch, I suppose, hoping someone would see the light, till the battery failed. Heavens, what am I to do about this? How can he be a prisoner?

Harry waved reassuringly to the boy, and was just about to begin climbing down the tree when he saw that the prisoner had disappeared very suddenly indeed from the window. Then a furious face appeared and looked out. It was the face of a bearded man with big glasses, rimmed with black.

Harry slid out of sight at once. He climbed down as quickly as he could and told the others what he had seen. They listened breathlessly.

'Then it *is* an adventure,' said Dick. 'I had a feeling we were in for one. We'll have to rescue this boy. Perhaps he has been kidnapped.'

'Yes. I never thought of that,' said Harry. 'We'd better look in the paper and see if there's anything about kidnapping. We never look at the paper in the usual way, so we wouldn't know.'

They went back to the cottage, and on the way they met Mrs Harriman, going to clean at the old house.

'Mrs Harriman – have you seen the man at the house?' asked Harry. 'Is he all alone?'

'Yes, not a soul there besides himself,' said the charwoman. 'Says he's writing a book and has to be quiet and by himself.'

'Are you sure there's nobody else?' asked Dick. 'Have you been all over the house?'

'Course I have,' said Mrs Harriman. 'Not on the top floor, though, because there's nothing there, so Mr Cordery says.'

'Oh – that's what he says, is it?' said Harry. 'Well, Mrs Harriman – just suppose I told you there was a prisoner up there!'

Mrs Harriman laughed loudly. 'Now don't you go playing any more of your jokes on me, young Harry. I've had enough of them. If you think you're going to make me climb up those steep stairs to the top, just to look for an imaginary prisoner, well, you can think again. You and your imagination!'

And she went on her way, chuckling. It was no good trying to get any advice from Mrs Harriman, or any help either! They went in at their cottage gate, and looked for the paper.

And there headlines, big and black, stared them in the face. 'Jackie Macario, son of famous film star, kidnapped.' The children gazed at them as if they couldn't believe their eyes.

'Do you think,' said Cathy at last, in a whisper, 'do you think that's the boy – the one Harry saw?'

'Yes,' said Dick. 'Miss Truman, did you see

this in the paper this morning – about the kidnapping? Well, we know where the boy is.'

'Now, don't tell silly stories,' said Miss Truman, placidly. 'If you want to pretend things and play games like that, you can – but really you can't expect me to believe them!'

And the more the children told her about what they knew, the more she pooh-poohed it all. She could not realize that they were no longer small children, and she wasn't going to be bothered to go into their ridiculous tales.

'It's no good,' said Harry, at last. 'We'd better do something ourselves. We'll rescue him tonight!'

'How?' asked Dick at once.

'We'll go through the underground passage, into the cellar, up into the kitchen, and up to the top floor,' said Harry. 'The door will be locked and bolted – but the key and bolt will be on the outside, and we can easily undo them!'

'Oh – I'd be afraid!' said Cathy.

'Well, don't come then,' said Dick. 'I'll go along with Harry – and we'll take Kim too.'

'Oh no, I *must* come if you go,' said Cathy bravely. So they laid their plans, and waited anxiously for the night to come.

At eleven o'clock they set out, with their torches. Kim went with them. He had been warned not to bark, and he quite understood.

The three children came to the little tumble-down summer-house and removed the flagstone that hid the entrance underground. Down they went, one by one. Cathy was trembling. It was so dark and strange. She was glad to feel Kim's tongue on her bare legs now and then.

Along the passage – up to the cellar – up the wooden steps to the vast dark kitchen, where a winking red eye showed where the great range was almost out. Then out of the kitchen and into the hall.

The wide stairs lay before them, well carpeted. Where was Mr Cordery? In bed, probably. There was no light to be seen anywhere.

The three went up the stairs with Kim beside them. It seemed as if he, too, was walking on tiptoe! Up one flight of stairs – up another – and then a third. Now they were at the very top of the house.

Harry swung his torch around the top landing. All the doors were open but one. In that one must be the prisoner!

They tiptoed towards it. It was bolted. There was a large key in the lock, and the children felt sure the door was locked too.

Cautiously Harry turned the key. It gave a slight click. Then he slid back the bolt. It creaked a little, and the children held their breath as they waited to see if anyone had heard. No, there was no sound.

Harry turned the handle and pushed the door open. The room was in darkness. Then a scared voice came from somewhere. 'Oh, what do you want? Why do you keep me here like this? Don't hurt me, don't hurt me!'

It was a boy's voice. Harry switched on his torch and spoke in a whisper.

'Are you Jackie Macario?'

'Yes, yes. Who are you? Oh, don't scare me so!'

'We are your friends,' said Harry. 'We've come to rescue you. I'm the boy you saw in the tree – the one you showed those letters to.'

'Oh, yes – I got beaten for that,' said the boy. 'Have you really come to rescue me? Let's go then, before that horrible man discovers you.'

Without waiting to put on even a dressing gown the boy went to the door with the others. He jumped violently when Kim licked him for he had not known there was a dog there.

'It's only Kim,' whispered Dick. 'Come on. Down the stairs.'

They went down the stairs as quietly as possible. But suddenly, in the darkness, Cathy bumped into something and it fell over with a crash. Scared almost out of their skin, the four children ran swiftly across the landing to the next flight of stairs.

And then suddenly a door was flung open, a light flashed on, and there was Mr Cordery, black-bearded and fierce, glaring at them in the greatest astonishment.

'What's this? Who are you? Come here, you, you, you . . .'

He was in such a rage that he could not get his words out. He caught hold of Dick and shook him like a rat.

The others paused, afraid for Dick. Kim gave a growl and flung himself on Mr Cordery. The man gave a shout and tried to fend the dog away. 'Come on, Dick!' shouted Harry, running down the next flight of stairs. 'Leave Kim to settle him.' They had enough time to dart into the kitchen. Then Kim came after them, his head bleeding from a savage blow. Then came Mr Cordery raging with temper, an iron bar in his hand. The children ran to the cellar-door and down the wooden steps. Kim followed them.

The door slammed above them. They heard Mr Cordery's loud laugh. 'Ha! You want to be prisoners, too, do you? Well, you shall all stay down in the cellar, in the dark and cold, with the spiders and the bats!'

Then the key turned in the lock of the cellar-door. Harry began to laugh weakly. 'He thinks we're his prisoners. He doesn't know it's our way of escape. Come on, quick, before he smells a rat!'

They dragged the surprised and frightened

boy with them. Down the steps, into the under-ground cellar, along the passage and up into the old summer-house. Then through the woods and home. Cathy was terribly worried about poor Kim. Was he very badly hurt?

They went into the house and banged on Miss Truman's door. 'Miss Truman! Come quickly!'

Miss Truman came, looking most astonished. When she saw the three bedraggled children, and a fourth one, quite strange to her, and poor Kim bleeding from his wound, she was filled with amazement.

The children poured out everything to her. 'Oh dear, oh dear, why didn't you tell me before?' she said, as she bathed Kim's head.

'But we *did*, and you thought we were making it all up,' said Cathy, quite crossly. 'Miss Truman, oughtn't we to tell the police? Jackie Macario's mother and father ought to know where he is, and the police ought to know about Mr Cordery.'

'Of course, of course,' said Miss Truman, putting her arm round the shivering Jackie. 'You go and get a dressing-gown for him, Harry. Kim will be all right now. I'll go and phone. Dear me, what a night, what a night! I can scarcely believe it!'

Neither could the policeman when Miss Truman telephoned to him. But he did believe her tale at last, and said he would telephone to his superior officer in the next town and get instructions.

And before very long a police car came roaring up with three big policemen in it, all very anxious to see for themselves if the little prisoner the children had rescued really and truly *was* Jackie Macario.

Nobody had much sleep that night, except little Jackie, who was tired out with excitement.

The police left the cottage and roared on to the old house. Mr Cordery was astounded to hear loud knockings on the front door, and only when he heard that it was the police who were demanding entrance did he open the door.

And then it was Mr Cordery who was taken prisoner! 'I tell you I know nothing about Jackie Macario,' he kept saying. 'Nothing at all.'

But when he was faced with the boy the next day, he could no longer go on with his tale. 'All right,' he said, suddenly. 'I'll tell you everything, see? I didn't kidnap him – the others did that. I brought him here and put him in that barred room to wait till the ransom was paid. That's all I did. And then some interfering kids got him away – though how they got into the house – and out of the cellar I locked them into, beats me!'

'Yes. A clever lot of kids,' said the Inspector, smiling round at the three children. 'Well,

Jackie, your parents will soon be here, and you'll be safe again.'

'I'd like to stay with these children if Mother will let me,' said Jackie. But alas, she wouldn't. She took her precious son away with her, thankful to have him safely back – but she left behind three things that thrilled the children tremendously.

One was a great rubber ball for playing about with on the beach or in the sea. That was for Harry.

Another was a shrimping net almost as big as the one the fishermen used when they went shrimping. That was for Dick.

The third was a funny rubber horse that could be ridden in the waves. That was for Cathy.

'Gracious!' said Cathy, in delight. 'What fantastic presents – and all for taking part in a really thrilling adventure. Miss Truman, you can have a ride on my horse if you like, next time you bathe.'

'No, *thank* you,' said Miss Truman, eyeing the big rubber creature in horror. 'I know what would happen to me! I'd be pushed off it at once – that would be your idea of a joke!'

The children laughed and raced off to the beach with their presents. 'Let's hope for another adventure soon!' said Dick. 'They're FUN!'

UNCLE CLEANS UP

J. P. Martin

After Uncle's great victory over the Badfort crowd, he felt he could look forward to a peaceful summer. Uncle and his supporters had driven off Beaver Hateman and his gang after a fierce fight, and now was a time of celebration — of fireworks and banquets and messages of congratulation.

'I really think we've dealt with them this time,' he said. But the Old Monkey, his faithful friend and helper, was not so sure. . .

UNCLE CLEANS UP is the second book about the fantastical adventures of that extraordinary elephant, Uncle and his friends.

The Sparrow Bookshop

Sparrow has a whole nestful of exciting books that are available in bookshops or that you can order by post through the Sparrow Bookshop. Just complete the form below and enclose the money due and the books will be sent to you at home.

THE SECRET OF LOST LAKE	Carolyn Keene	95p ☐
THE WINKING RUBY MYSTERY	Carolyn Keene	£1.00 ☐
THE GHOST IN THE GALLERY	Carolyn Keene	£1.00 ☐
STAR TREK SHORT STORIES	William Rotsler	£1.00 ☐
A PONY FOUND	D. Pullein-Thompson	95p ☐
SAVE THE PONIES	J. Pullein-Thompson	£1.00 ☐
A NIGHT ON THUNDER ROCK	Enid Blyton	95p ☐
DRACULA	Bram Stoker	95p ☐

Humour

FUNNIEST JOKE BOOK	Jim Eldridge	£1.00 ☐
BROWNIE JOKE BOOK	Compiled by Brownies	95p ☐
SCHOOL FOR LAUGHS	Peter Eldin	95p ☐
NOT TO BE TAKEN SERIOUSLY	Colin West	£1.00 ☐

And if you would like to hear more about our forthcoming books, write to the address below for the Sparrow News.

SPARROW BOOKS, BOOKSERVICE BY POST, PO BOX 29, DOUGLAS, ISLE OF MAN, BRITISH ISLES.

Please enclose a cheque or postal order made out to Arrow Books Limited for the amount due including 8p per book for postage and packing for orders within the UK and 10p for overseas orders.

Please print clearly

NAME...

ADDRESS ....

....

Whilst every effort is made to keep prices down and popular books in print, Arrow Books cannot guarantee that prices will be the same as those advertised here or that the books will be available.